The world is in peril.

An ancient evil is rising from beneath Erdas, and we need YOU to help stop it.

Claim your spirit animal and join the adventure now:

1. Go to scholastic.com/spiritanimals.

2. Log in to create your character and choose your own spirit animal.

3. Have your book ready and enter the code below to unlock the adventure.

Your code: NMW2FHJRWF

By the Four Fallen,
The Greencloaks

scholastic.com/spiritanimals

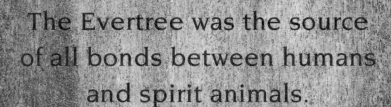

The Evertree was the source
of all bonds between humans
and spirit animals.

And there was no mistaking it:
The tree was dying.

FALL of the BEASTS
SPIRIT ANIMALS

IMMORTAL
GUARDIANS

Eliot Schrefer

SCHOLASTIC INC.

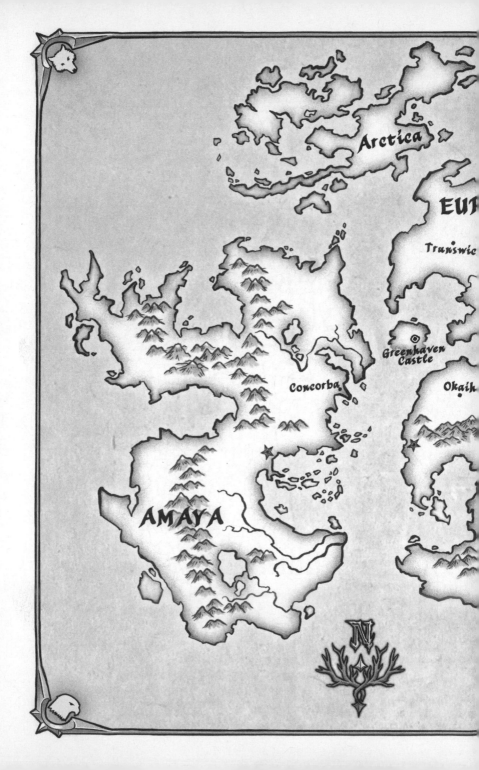

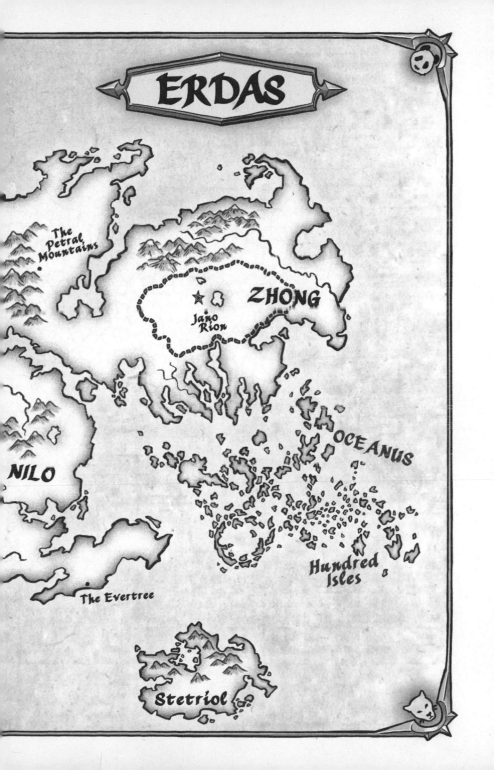

Library of Congress Control Number: 2015940289

ISBN 978-0-545-87694-0

10 9 8 7 6 5 4 3 2 1   15 16 17 18 19

Book design by Charice Silverman
Library edition, August 2015

Printed in the U.S.A.   23

Scholastic US: 557 Broadway • New York, NY 10012
Scholastic Canada: 604 King Street West • Toronto, ON • M5V 1E1
Scholastic New Zealand Limited: Private Bag 94407 • Greenmount, Manukau 2141
Scholastic UK Ltd.: Euston House • 24 Eversholt Street • London NW1 1DB

IMMORTAL
GUARDIANS

MARKET DAY

IF ONLY SHE COULD TURN RIGHT AROUND AND GO HOME. Normally Kaiina lived with her tribe, day in and day out—she hadn't been around this many unknown people for years, not since she had once come with her mother to this very marketplace as a little girl. But she was twelve now, which meant she'd have to start taking her turn trekking to the jungle market to buy supplies for her tribe.

Everyone had requests. Oranges for her father. A new hunting blade for her mother. Sugarfruit for her brother.

Thinking of how happy her family would be with their presents gave Kaiina the courage she needed. Holding her head high, she stepped into the clearing.

She picked her way between the woven mats, perusing the goods carefully laid out on each. Fragrant herbs, wild pineapple and celery, grouse eggs—her stomach growled as she passed among the vendors. To prevent herself from wasting her tribe's money, she recited her short list in her mind, like a mantra. *Oranges. A hunting blade. Sugarfruit.*

Vendors beckoned to Kaiina as she passed, but she timidly avoided their eyes. She'd never bartered before and was worried they'd take advantage of her the moment she showed interest in what they were selling.

"Kaiina!"

She looked up, startled, and was relieved to see a familiar old woman scamper agilely through the crowded vendor mats and come to Kaiina's side, warmly taking the girl's hands in her own. Kaiina relaxed: Prana was an elderly woman who traveled between the tribes, bartering her pottery. Kaiina had known her for years, and had never seen Prana without a smile on her old, cracked face.

Prana's spirit animal, a brilliant brass kingfisher, was perched on the woman's long gray braid, its delicate feet hooked into the folds of silvered hair. The bird hopped to Kaiina's shoulder, warbling a cheerful, tuneless song.

I wish I had a spirit animal, Kaiina thought. *Then I'd always have company, and wouldn't have to come to market day alone.* But some people bonded with spirit animals and some didn't—there was no predicting it. And Kaiina hadn't summoned one.

"He is not usually this excited to see anyone—he really likes you!" Prana said.

Kaiina took a moment to run her hand over the bird's smooth and glossy plumage. He raised his chin, inviting her to preen his underfeathers. Kaiina smiled and obliged.

Just then, Prana's kingfisher took to the air and began to shriek. From all around, the trees shook. Monkeys screamed. Cicadas droned. Songbirds chattered.

Kaiina felt a strange dizzy sensation wash over her, and the market fell into silence.

The ground seemed to tilt beneath Kaiina's bare feet. "What is happening?" she cried out.

Though only moments before she'd been so hot she was sweating, Kaiina shivered with a sudden chill. The sky went dark, and the clouds turned rageful and knitted together. She heard a boom and a crack, and her eyes filled with light.

The explosion knocked Kaiina and Prana to the ground. Ears ringing, Kaiina's first thought was to help the elderly woman up. But Prana was already back on her feet, tears in her rheumy eyes. Blinking her own eyes rapidly to clear the purple flash, Kaiina raised herself onto her elbows.

As quickly as they'd formed, the clouds scattered. The clearing was once again full of radiant sunshine, its brilliance frosting the silhouette of a giant creature where just moments before there had been nothing.

"It is not possible," Prana whispered. But it was. An elephant had appeared.

The massive beast bowed its head, trunk slung low and snuffling along the ground. Kaiina had seen plenty of forest elephants in the jungle, but none as big as this one. Its broad ears swayed as it made its way toward Kaiina and Prana. Vendors and tribespeople alike fled to the edges of the market, watching with fearful curiosity.

Kaiina's legs were rooted to the ground.

"D-do you know this elephant?" she stammered to Prana. "Where did it come from? And why is it coming toward you?"

"Not toward *me*, child," Prana said, wonder in her voice. "It's coming toward *you*."

"I don't understand!" Kaiina cried, tears blurring her vision.

"You've summoned a spirit animal," Prana said. She had placed a wizened hand over her mouth, making her words almost inaudible. "But an elephant, the eyes . . . it's impossible! Kaiina, you've summoned Dinesh."

Dinesh? A creature of legend, one of the Great Beasts of Erdas? It felt as if the earth went soft beneath Kaiina, as if she'd stepped into slipmud.

The elephant slowed as it came near, and Kaiina was shocked to see it lower its great head. Brilliant aqua eyes met hers, and they flashed with intelligence and something almost like amusement as they took in the cowering marketgoers. Could this animal truly be the great Dinesh?

"Say hello," Prana encouraged. "He's waiting to meet you."

The creature's expression softened, and Kaiina found her legs were able to move again. Despite the dozens of eyes she could feel on her back, despite the ruckus of the upturned earth and the bizarre sight of an enormous elephant standing on the woven mats, Kaiina didn't shrink away. She *wanted* to touch him. A charge was building up inside her, setting her skin tingling, and she knew instinctively that only one thing would settle it.

Hands trembling, she strode to the elephant and leaned in close so their faces were mere inches apart. As she ran the back of her hand along his leathery ear and closed her eyes, a serene warmth filled her.

Kaiina felt a moist touch on her neck. Opening her eyes, she smiled as she saw that Dinesh's large trunk was nuzzling her. *Comforting* her. Suddenly she felt as large as the elephant, somehow—too large to be intimidated by a crowded marketplace. It seemed ridiculous that she'd ever been.

Kaiina hesitantly laid a hand against the elephant's flank. His flesh was rough and thick, his giant torso rising and falling beneath her fingers. She looked into the elephant's eyes and saw a vast intelligence gazing back.

"How could I have summoned Dinesh?" Kaiina asked in wonder. "And why to *me*?"

Before Prana could answer, a man in a black tunic stepped forward. "This is indeed an auspicious morning!" the stranger called. "The Great Beasts are returning, and I have been sent to shepherd them to safety."

Prana's golden kingfisher pointed his sharp beak shrewdly at the man. Kaiina's attention was drawn to the charcoal-colored spiral on the man's forehead. She could see now that it was raised and swollen, more of a brand than a tattoo. It almost appeared to ripple in the wavering heat, but after the shock of the last few moments, Kaiina wasn't sure she could trust her senses. She leaned into Dinesh's side for security, and took comfort in the slow rise and fall of his ribs.

"You may leave the girl and her elephant in my care, old one. I will handle it from here."

The elephant raised his trunk into the air, letting out a deep trumpeting call, the sound powerful enough to reverberate deep in Kaiina's chest. From elsewhere in the jungle, other elephants called in response. When she heard distant crashing sounds, Kaiina realized the other elephants were converging on them.

Dinesh tossed his head in the stranger's direction, lowering his tusks and leveling them toward the man in the black tunic. Kaiina stroked Dinesh's ear and saw that the elephant's eyes were full of distrust.

"Kalistan-ah," Kaiina whispered to Prana in the local language. *Beware.*

Before Prana could respond, the stranger stepped toward them. He was handsome and tan-skinned, a trim beard covering his jaw. *"Sia-ga,"* he said, a wicked grin splitting his face, "I speak your language, and yes, you should be afraid."

The treetops again began to shake, and the nearby monkeys and birds recommenced their shrieking. The cicadas went from a low drone to a roar. Kaiina looked to Dinesh, hoping to discover in the elephant's soft eyes that she had nothing to fear. But fear was precisely what Kaiina found there.

Dinesh took a step forward and then a step back, lowering his head nervously. Kaiina followed his gaze and saw a thicket of spiny jungle growth tremble and shake. As the branches bent farther and whatever creature was behind them began to emerge, Dinesh trumpeted again.

"What's wrong?" Kaiina cried out. The powerful vibration of the elephant's call rattled in her head.

Marketgoers had begun to approach from their safe vantage, but paused after they heard the elephant's trumpet. It was a good thing they did, too, as Dinesh suddenly charged. They scurried to get out of the way, but the elephant was only halfway across the clearing when he abruptly halted, momentum hurtling his body through the dirt and nearly pitching him forward.

Emerging from the thicket was another huge creature. It was a bear, but unlike any Kaiina had ever seen. She'd been taught that bears were always brown or black, but this one was white, its fur as light as morning clouds against the vibrant blacks and greens of the jungle. Baffled, Kaiina wheeled and caught Prana's startled eyes.

"What wrongness has come to our world?" Prana cried, her hand to her heart.

There was a cry from the sky, and a large eagle descended, lowering so it was flapping above the polar bear. Then there was a roar from the other side of the clearing, and Kaiina pivoted to see a giant boar, thick-tusked and bristly.

Blinded by fear, Kaiina ran toward Prana but was blocked by a new creature—this one a muscular beast on all fours, like a stocky antelope, but with curling horns on its head. It used those horns to butt into Prana, who staggered and fell before Kaiina's eyes. Her kingfisher hovered, trying ineffectually to stop the beast's assault.

Kaiina backed up, hands outstretched as she sought the company of her newfound spirit animal. Dinesh wasn't hard to find, trumpeting and screaming as he whirled in the center of the clearing, facing off against both the polar bear and the boar. Standing calmly between the two attacking beasts was the stranger in the black tunic.

"Why are you doing this?" Kaiina cried.

The man didn't answer. Hearing Kaiina's distress, Dinesh pivoted to face her. With one clean motion he whipped his trunk around, caught the girl around the waist, and deposited her securely on his broad back. He immediately returned to fending off the bear and the boar, whipping his great tusks through the air to keep them at bay.

The stranger grinned at Kaiina. The spiral on his forehead was definitely moving now, writhing under his flesh. "Haven't you figured it out? I am collecting the Great Beasts. And Dinesh is my next trophy."

With that, the man pulled an obsidian vial out of a pouch at his waist and unstopped it. A feeling of cold dread passed through her.

The polar bear and the boar had spread out. The elephant turned in nervous circles. With the other Great Beasts flanking him, Dinesh could no longer fend off both attackers at once. Kaiina wondered how much longer his tusks would keep them safe.

With a rush of wind, the eagle was there. It hovered beside the bearded man, who placed the mysterious black vial in its talons. With a few flaps of its strong wings, the eagle flew up toward Kaiina. She cringed, clenching her legs tightly against Dinesh as she instinctively threw her arms before her face.

But the eagle wasn't coming for her.

Kaiina watched in horror as it dexterously turned the vial in its talons, letting the contents fall onto Dinesh's broad forehead. At first Kaiina thought it was a piece of gray mud inside, but then she saw the glob start moving, and realized it was a worm, or a leech—the same size and shape as the twisting spiral on the stranger's forehead. Kaiina leaned forward desperately, hoping to use the back of her hand to wipe the little monster off Dinesh.

But the worm was surprisingly fast. It wriggled over Dinesh's forehead, easily sticking to the elephant's hide, no matter how frantically he tried to shake it. The worm pressed its toothy sucker mouth against Dinesh time and again, but was clearly finding it hard to get through Dinesh's tough skin. Kaiina swatted at it, but the wriggling creature was too fast. It lurched for Dinesh's ear, soon disappearing in the folds. She realized how far it had gotten when she heard the elephant cry out in pain and shake his head furiously.

Dinesh began to tremble and shudder beneath Kaiina's thighs. He lifted his head and trumpeted one more time, a terrible, anguished cry. Then he went quiet and still.

The bear and the boar relented, stepping back from the elephant.

"Dinesh!" Kaiina yelled. Her hands were clamped on the elephant's head. "Are you okay? Dinesh!"

He was motionless.

"At least you had a few moments with your spirit animal," the man said. "Some I don't even give that much."

Kaiina rubbed the elephant's hide, hoping Dinesh would reawaken to her touch. But the electricity was gone, and the elephant remained still.

The boar relaxed and sat in the dirt while the bear panted heavily in the jungle heat, tongue lolling out of its mouth. Kaiina felt suddenly light-headed, like she might pass out from shock.

The stranger in black tugged at the length of rawhide that tied the collar of his shirt closed, exposing a broad chest. In the middle of it, right in the triangle where his abdomen began, was a tattoo of what looked like a cobra. The stranger closed his eyes, his brow wrinkling with concentration. Then, with a flash, the bear and boar had disappeared, appearing on the man's chest, one on either side, forelimbs reaching out onto the muscles of his shoulders. Kaiina heard popping sounds behind her and saw two more tattoos appear on the man's chest: an eagle and a ram. There was a large space left in the middle, right below his throat.

"No, no . . ." Kaiina moaned, realization dawning.

"Oh, but yes," the man said, his voice a low purr.

There was another flash, this one right below her, and suddenly Kaiina was falling. She fell hard onto the muddy ground, the breath knocked out of her. Wheezing and shaking, she raised herself on her hands and saw a new tattoo in the center of the man's chest, riding over his breastbone. Dinesh.

"Who are you?" Kaiina gasped. "Why have you done this?"

The man loomed over her, crossing his arms over the animal tattoos on his powerful chest. The strange spiral brand on the man's face writhed. He winced as the flesh on his forehead puckered and stretched. His eyes took on a dim glow, became the color of twilight.

"The whole world knew my name once, and soon it will know it again. I am Zerif."

THE EVERTREE

I**T WAS A BREEZY, BEAUTIFUL DAY, AND THE EVERTREE WAS** singing. As the wind passed through its leaves, they tinkled together and played a song as chaotic and joyous as a burbling stream. Lenori raised her hands to the sunshine and closed her eyes, taking in the magnificence of the moment.

Part of her wished she could stay here forever.

Back in Greenhaven, Lenori had kept a simple herb garden. She'd loved the daily labor of it—running her fingers through silky black soil, picking just the right spot to place each batch of seeds. She supposed that growing plants wasn't that unlike training the new Greencloak recruits. When a child summoned a spirit animal and joined the ancient order, it had been Lenori who would care for them. Not just their training, but their hearts and well-being, too—something blustery Olvan often overlooked.

But all the same, when she'd lived in Greenhaven, Lenori had often found herself taking long walks along misty battlements, looking down longingly on a forest world that seemed all too far away. She'd never quite taken to gray stone walls.

Her new job taking care of the Evertree was much more suited to her.

For generations, it had been the secret source of the spirit animal bond—perhaps the source of life itself on Erdas. But the world fell into war. Kovo the Ape, one of the Great Beasts, betrayed his brethren in a bid to control the Evertree. During the resulting conflict, it had been destroyed.

Then, through a miracle that Lenori had yet to fully understand, after the Great Beasts sacrificed themselves, the tree was born anew.

Above her, the Great Tree's branches groaned in the wind. Its golden leaves rustled, their song growing louder.

How beautiful the tree was! Every day its splendor grew. The height of a mountain, its great silver spire rose so tall that its highest branches stroked the clouds, generating a constant patter of rain on the ground below. After its first months of rapid growth, the tree had begun to sprout golden leaves, each an intricately wrought marvel, as delicate as the finest filigree, fanning out from the elegant arcs of the tree's branches. The Evertree changed colors according to the sun's mood, going from silver-white at dawn to blazing yellow at midday, then maturing to muted, steely afternoons and purple explosions at sunset. Living with the tree was the opposite of lonely, not when Lenori had that magnificent canopy above her. And of course there was also Myriam, her rainbow ibis companion.

In Greenhaven she'd been a vain, preening creature, taking great pains to arrange her feathers just so, ensuring that every color of the rainbow was on display somewhere on her body. But now Myriam was too busy playing host to worry about that—the ibis kept busy greeting each newly arriving bird as Lenori made her long daily trek around the vast trunk of the Evertree. Myriam would join Lenori at camp at the end of each day, snacking on a few tasty bugs from the mud before plopping down beside Lenori's bedroll, exhausted.

One day, though, Myriam hadn't come to her before sunset. That was unusual, but not much cause for concern; some new peacocks had recently arrived at the tree, and Myriam had spent the day following them around, keeping tabs on which was the most beautiful. When Lenori finally tracked Myriam down, she found her staring at a patch of bark along one of the tree's silvery exposed roots.

Lenori knelt beside the ibis and stroked her spirit animal's iridescent plumage. Her focus remained on the tree. Lenori looked where she was staring, and her heart stuttered.

Rot.

It was a patch no longer than her finger, as purple-gray as a bruise on a pear. When Lenori tentatively pressed her finger to the blemish, she found it was soft, squishing beneath her touch with a wet, sighing sound.

She'd never considered that the Evertree could be susceptible to the same minor infections that plagued all trees. Lenori examined it for any other signs of illness, but the Evertree was shining and healthy. As she lay down in her bedroll that evening, her thoughts were on that strange black mark.

The next day Myriam kept close to Lenori's side, hopping along the shady ground, never more than a few feet away, even ignoring the upstart peacocks when they brazenly strutted by. When Lenori returned to the spot where she had last seen the rot, she held her breath.

And let it out in a sharp gasp.

The patch had grown. When Lenori placed her hand over the root, the blemish was the size of her middle three fingers. She tentatively tried to peel the rotten bark away, and when the black sludgy paper came free in her fingers, she saw there was a crevice behind the rot, a black arc slicing into the tree's pristine silver.

Lenori had grown up in the mangrove forests of Amaya and knew a few tricks for curing tree rot. She gathered lichen and wedged it into the narrow black crack, wetting the patch with pond water. Lichen had its own ways of fighting invaders and could work like a poultice to stave off this black sickness, if the Evertree couldn't manage it on its own.

But when Lenori next returned, the lichen had withered and the rot was bigger. It was as big as *her* now, a Lenori-sized patch of decay along a root of the tree. It loomed over her, like an accusation.

Lenori stepped toward the rot reaching up the trunk. As usual, she tested it with her fingers, removing whatever bits of black mush she could, hoping to slow the infection's progress. This time, when she pressed against the rot, it gave way with a soft tearing sound. Her arm passed right into the humid space behind.

Lenori ripped away at the cavity, heedless of the black goo caking her arms and face. The dead bark was like a curtain, hiding an empty space that extended back into the tree. She took a tentative step into it and gasped.

The rot must have been eating at the tree for a long time, longer than Lenori had known. She was in a cavern that led deep into the tree, bits of dying wood dropping around her. Everywhere was the strangely sweet smell of death and rot, and the soft slimy blackness of the Evertree's sickness.

Looking down, Lenori saw that the rotten hollow extended down, into caverns and dank tunnels under the earth.

The Evertree was the source of all bonds between humans and spirit animals. If it fell, those partnerships would cease to exist.

And there was no mistaking it: The tree was dying.

HOMECOMING

MEILIN WAITED IMPATIENTLY ON THE DOCKS. ITCHING TO ascend the path to Greenhaven and greet her friends, she massaged a knot of worry that had appeared at the back of her neck. That knot was an old friend—it had shown up during the war, and only left her after months of peace spent in Zhong, undertaking the simple, satisfying work of rebuilding a nation stone by stone. But now that she'd gotten word of Erdas's new troubles, the knot was back.

She flexed her dominant arm while she waited, hoping she hadn't gotten too soft during her time home.

Greencloaks were coming and going along the docks, whispering among themselves and cutting admiring glances at Meilin. Meilin had more self-assurance than most twelve-year-olds, or most adults for that matter, but it made her nervous to be seen as a hero. In Zhong, she'd perfected a serene smile, warm enough to honor the person's interest but chilly enough to discourage handshakes and questions.

"Aren't you done yet?" Meilin asked the guard imperiously.

She'd been ready to drag her trunk right up to the hulking castle of Greenhaven, but a young Greencloak had stopped her along the path. He'd apologized and then started searching Meilin's trunk, meticulously picking through her things.

"Find any hidden weapons?" Meilin asked.

"I'm sorry, ma'am," the guard said, embarrassed. "We're required to search everyone arriving in Greenhaven. After the war . . ."

"Yes, yes. I remember the war, believe me." It had only brought Meilin the title of Hero of Erdas. It had only caused her to bond to a Great Beast. It had only killed her father.

The guard turned bright crimson as he got to the last layer of Meilin's case: underwear. "I don't suppose you suspect I've hidden any killer crocodiles in those?" Meilin asked, peeking over his shoulder.

Jhi, a giant panda, made a warning grunt where she was sitting a few feet away and philosophically chewing on a piece of bamboo. Lately Jhi had started to take Meilin to task whenever she slipped into rudeness. It was very annoying.

Suddenly aware that her arms were crossed over her chest and her nose was raised haughtily, Meilin forced herself to smile at the guard. "I, um, like your turkey."

The man's spirit animal, a particularly unimpressive fowl that was ecstatically picking worms out of a nearby leaf pile, raised its head, shook its wattle, then returned its attention to the dirt.

The guard finished his search, his face still crimson while he stuffed Meilin's underwear back in her trunk as fast as he could. "Sorry for the delay, ma'am," he said. "Everyone gets searched, even the Four Heroes of Erdas."

"You can make it up to me by carrying my case," Meilin said. Jhi grunted again. "Oh, fine, I'll get it myself."

Meilin and Jhi began the walk up the long and winding path to Greenhaven castle, an imposing gray stone structure that rose high over the sea. Though it was an intimidating place, Meilin felt an unexpected joy when she saw it. Greenhaven was as much her home as Zhong. All the same—if she'd had her way, she might never have come back.

Rollan, she thought as she scanned the ramparts of the imposing stone fortress the Greencloaks called home. *Where are you?*

She'd known the situation was serious when Rollan sent his own spirit animal to call her back from Zhong. She'd been ready to bunk down for the night after a long day helping build a new bridge for the capital when the falcon had rushed into her cabin. A small golden tube had been banded to one of Essix's legs.

Even in her exhaustion, the falcon had managed a disdainful look as Meilin unscrewed the top of the cylinder and tugged out a rolled-up letter. Meilin had imagined what Essix would say if she could: *Essix the Falcon is not a messenger pigeon! Essix eats messenger pigeons for breakfast!*

The note had been ominously short.

Meilin,

I know you had to spend some time away for your sanity, and I'm not asking this lightly. But you must come to Greenhaven as soon as you can. Evertree in danger. Will explain when you get here.

—Your Rollan

Rollan had once described the feeling of being far from the gyrfalcon as having someone scratch at his eyelids. Sending Essix all the way to Zhong must have been excruciating. Meilin couldn't wait to see her friend's face when he was reunited with his spirit animal. She couldn't wait to see his face in general, actually.

Essix had flown on ahead as soon as Meilin's boat arrived, but now returned, alighting on Meilin's shoulder with a squawk of delight. Then, with a shriek, Meilin was bowled over by an unseen assailant. She panicked for a moment, before she felt the long, stinky licks of a wolf's rough tongue on her cheek.

"Briggan!" she cried, laughing with joy through her tears as she wrapped her arms around the wolf's neck. "Conor!" she shouted, hoping Briggan's human partner was nearby. "Where are you? Get this oversized dog off me!"

But Briggan kept licking, and before she knew it Meilin was joined on the ground by her friends Abeke, Conor, and then Rollan, laughing and hugging as they rolled on the flagstones of the path, heedless of the scene they were making.

One of the Greencloaks making his way up the path giggled, and the phrase *"Four Heroes of Erdas"* passed through Meilin's mind. She remembered her dignity and stood up, primly brushing soil and grass from her traveling clothes.

Rollan stayed on the ground and looked up at her, ripping up a handful of grass and adding it to the bits already dusting his shiny, unkempt hair. Meilin's heart kicked when she saw that the lean Amayan boy looked just the same, with his dark hair and impish grin. At least some things hadn't changed during her time in Zhong.

"Embarrassed to be seen with us, milady?" Rollan joked. Essix landed neatly on his shoulder.

Conor smudged some mud on Rollan's nose, then busted into a guffaw. "*Now* she'll be embarrassed of you."

Abeke turned serious before the boys did. The tall Niloan girl brushed herself off, too, and stood shoulder-to-shoulder with Meilin. She pointed up at Greenhaven castle. "I'd hoped we could give you the time off you wanted—we wouldn't have called you back unless we had to, I promise. Let's head up to the castle. I'll explain on the way."

Abeke took one handle of Meilin's trunk, and together they started up toward the fortress. Abeke's leopard, Uraza, and Jhi kept pace with them, the boys and their spirit animals tailing behind. Abeke had clearly been practicing her fighting skills while Meilin was off helping rebuild Zhong; as they walked Meilin admired the bands of muscle lining the Niloan girl's arms. Even the bow on Abeke's back looked heavier than the one she'd previously used. But Meilin knew what her friend would really want her opinion on. "I like your new skinnier braids," Meilin said to Abeke.

"Really?" Abeke said, her hand unconsciously going to her hair. Abeke toyed with the wooden bead at the end of a braid, then let it fall. "I've been experimenting. It was good while it lasted. There won't be time to worry about hairstyles anymore. Not now."

When Abeke started telling Meilin about recent events, all thoughts of hairstyles vanished from her mind.

"Great Beasts summoned as spirit animals, the Evertree sick—that can't be a coincidence," Meilin murmured.

"You think?" Rollan said sarcastically. "We managed to figure that much out, too."

"You can see why we wanted you back here," Abeke said.

"Of course," Meilin said gravely. A stony weight settled in her stomach. "What does Olvan have to say about all of this?" Meilin asked. The leader of the Greencloaks was their best source of wisdom.

"He went to check on Lenori at the Evertree. Due back any day. But wait," Abeke said. "You haven't heard the worst part."

Conor gave an involuntary shiver and wrapped a hand around his sleeve, pinning it to his arm. As if to hide something.

"What's going on?" Meilin asked.

"Surprise," Rollan said flatly, pointing ahead of them.

Meilin's gaze snapped forward. She dropped her side of the trunk. It fell against the flagstones, the wood splintering. "No! Oh no. What have we done?"

They'd arrived at the main courtyard of Greenhaven. It had none of its usual bustle, and even Mustado's familiar merchant stall was shuttered. Armed guards had been stationed on the battlements, all facing down into the courtyard. The reason was very clear. Chained in the center was an ape. Not just any ape: a gorilla.

The beast's rounded shoulders were what Meilin saw first. Broad stretches of pure muscle were covered in coarse black hair that turned silver where it trailed down his back. He stood on all fours, knuckles pressing heavily into the ground. The gorilla's noble, squared brow was held as proudly as possible, but a collar had been fitted around his neck, and the chain didn't reach quite high enough for him to raise his head. The ape was hunched, eyes scrunched tight, as if by squinting he could shut out the discomfort of his imprisonment.

"Tell me that's not Kovo," Meilin whispered.

"It is," Conor spat. "He's back."

"Summoned as a spirit animal," Abeke said, with a sighing sympathy in her voice. "Just like ours."

"*That's* the one Great Beast we managed to rescue?" Meilin asked. "The traitor?"

"He's smaller than before, at least," Rollan said. "Mini-Kovo."

"He is plenty big enough, thank you," Meilin said, refusing to take another step toward their sworn enemy. "Who summoned him?"

Her eyes lit on a skinny boy dressed in a stiff blue cotton robe drawn tight with a white sash. He was cross-legged on the ground, hunched like Kovo, his face in a motionless frown. Like the ape, he looked like he was focusing all his energy on surviving his current torment.

"Whoever is going around stealing the Great Beasts didn't manage to sever that boy's bond to Kovo?" Meilin asked.

"We got to him first," Abeke whispered. "Thanks to Conor. Takoda was raised by monks in a monastery in Southern Nilo. One of the monks was a Greencloak, fortunately. After Kovo appeared, she kept Takoda safely locked away while Conor rushed down to bring them back to Greenhaven."

Conor blushed slightly. "They were already under attack when I got there," he said. "I was lucky to get them out at all."

"*Who* was attacking?" Meilin asked. "I don't understand who could do this. Are there still Conquerors out there?"

Conor stared furiously at the ground, hand tight on his sleeve again. "It was Zerif," he said.

Meilin stared between her friends, anger rising within her. She knew that name. Zerif was a war criminal. One of the cruelest and most cunning enemies they'd ever encountered. But he'd never held the power to take a spirit animal. No one did.

"But we got to Kovo first. And he's certainly not in a position to cause anyone any trouble now," Abeke said, looking at Kovo with something almost like sympathy.

As if in response, Kovo slowly opened his eyes . . . and found Meilin's. She had forgotten how startling their color was. At the sight of his scarlet irises, cold sweat broke out down her back. Much as she tried to calm her fear, her instincts told her one thing only: *Run.*

Meilin fought to master the urge to flee. She would *not* let her enemies control her.

The courtyard had fallen silent as Kovo roused. All eyes turned toward the gorilla. He took in the scene blankly, betraying no emotion on his face. After giving Meilin a long, scalding look, he slowly closed his eyes again.

Abeke cleared her throat. "Takoda," she called to the seated boy. "Do you want to meet Meilin? The one we were telling you about?"

Meilin tore her eyes away from Kovo's hulking form as the boy got to his feet and walked over, shaking the chill out of his legs and knees. He was about Rollan's height, but so thin that even his stiff cotton robes couldn't hide the narrowness of his frame. When he got near, Meilin became confused—though his skin was dark, his features seemed almost Zhongese. When he spoke, his accent was like anyone else from Southern Nilo.

"You must be Meilin of Zhong," he said, bowing his shaved head. "It's an honor to meet such a famed warrior."

"Oh," Meilin said, hoping the blush she felt wasn't showing. "Thank you."

"You're as polite as always, Takoda," Rollan said to the boy, a complicated expression on his face.

Takoda smiled, avoiding Rollan's eyes. "I'm not quite the person you imagined would summon a huge blood-thirsty gorilla, I'm sure."

Meilin shrugged and cracked her calloused knuckles. "I summoned a fluffy panda. Go figure."

24

"You aren't going to like what I'm about to say," Takoda said. "We've all lost much to Kovo in the past, and those wounds are not yet healed. Though he might have . . . behaved poorly before, I think Kovo is trying to help you."

"Kovo *help us*?" Meilin asked. Fury surged through her. "Help us like he *helped* the Devourer rampage across Erdas?" she spat. "As I recall, the last person he *helped* was cast aside like an old toy when he was no longer useful."

"Just let me show you," Takoda said. He took two slow steps back, then turned on his heel and strode toward the ape.

"Takoda, wait!" Abeke cried.

From the battlements above came the sound of drawing bowstrings and swords. Greencloak guards shouted in alarm.

Meilin launched forward on instinct, reaching her hand out to grab Takoda. But she cursed her softened instincts as her fingers reached him a moment too late, catching only the hem of his robe.

Kovo sprang.

For a creature so large, the ape was astonishingly fast. With a single push of his meaty palms against the cobblestones he was beside Takoda, red eyes blazing within the dark of his face. The ape's fiery gaze flipped from the boy to Meilin, and the sudden intensity of it took her breath away.

Despite herself, Meilin halted, dropping into a more defensive crouch. With another crashing leap Kovo was past Takoda—and bounding straight at her.

Then the chain caught, and Kovo's collar jerked him to a halt.

He nearly tumbled to the ground but caught himself just in time, straining against the collar, his face inches from hers. Meilin could feel the ape's breath rustling the ends of her hair. Kovo's teeth were bared. A few links of chain were all that kept her from death.

Meilin, you are a warrior. She narrowed her eyes.

"No, stop!" Takoda pushed himself between the two of them, his skinny arms waving frantically. "Please, just listen. Kovo doesn't want to fight!"

Takoda faced the gorilla, and with the boy between her and her enemy, Meilin allowed herself to rise from her defensive stance.

"Show them," Takoda pleaded to Kovo. "*Please.*"

The gorilla's eyes were still fixed on Meilin's, with every bit of the calculating menace that she remembered. A raw surge of hatred passed through her. She could barely control the urge to attack.

Kovo shoved a chained hand at Takoda, knocking the boy back a step. Takoda let his hand drop, opened his satchel, and took out a roll of papyrus and a piece of charcoal. He placed them both on the ground in front of Kovo.

Meilin's anger slowly drained as she watched Kovo take the charcoal in his powerful fingers, holding the tool with surprising delicacy. Avoiding their eyes, the ape concentrated on the papyrus and began to sketch.

"It's always the same picture," Takoda explained. "He even draws all the parts in the same order. It's like he's trying to get it all perfectly right. Like he's trying to capture something that's been seared into his mind."

The gorilla started with a jaw, and the fangs came next. At first Meilin thought Kovo was drawing an animal—the Great Serpent Gerathon, perhaps. But it soon became clear that the jaw wasn't attached to any creature. Instead, there were stones and grass in front of it, a rocky mountain behind, and a half moon in the sky above.

"Is it the fossil of a giant jaw?" Meilin asked.

Kovo dropped the charcoal and stared at her. Under the sudden onslaught of the ape's cruel red eyes, Meilin fell back a step before she could remember her poise. Holding her head high, Meilin watched the ape trace an arc in the air, then walk through it with two fingers of his other hand.

"It's not a fossil," Takoda explained. "It's a door. Wait, he's not done. There's one more part to it."

Finally taking his gaze away from Meilin, Kovo picked the charcoal back up. On top of the fanged door, positioned right in its center, he drew a strange, disquieting symbol.

A twisting spiral.

THE PORTAL

W HO'D EVER GIVEN DOORWAYS MUCH THOUGHT? BUT now they were all Abeke could think about. As she and her friends passed through Greenhaven's chilly stone corridors, Abeke found herself looking up at every frame and archway. Turned out that a doorway was never just a doorway. Some had shields hung above, some were splintered wood or gleaming granite, and some had frames of molding where there had once been glass.

None of Greenhaven's doorways looked even remotely like a set of fangs.

"No one has seen anything like it," Conor said forlornly, peering at the parchment with Kovo's charcoal drawing.

"It feels like we've asked nearly everyone in Greenhaven," Abeke said.

"Why not try the library?" Meilin asked.

The other three stared at her. "Greenhaven has a *library*?" Rollan asked.

Meilin rolled her eyes and led the way, bringing them down staircase after staircase. Natural light became scarce and then disappeared, replaced by the ruddy glow of guttering torches. "I came down here to study while we were training," she said. "Didn't you guys ever get the urge to pick up a book during training breaks?"

Abeke saw Conor blush and look away. In the last six months, he'd only just begun to learn how to read.

"Uh, yeah, of course," Rollan said dryly. "I was reading, like, all the time. The bigger the book, the better, that's what I always say."

"Someday our survival will rest on knowing all about ancient Hellan rock decorating, and you're going to thank me," Meilin said, cuffing him on the shoulder.

"Shh!" came a low, outraged voice.

They'd arrived at the library.

At the end of a dank, dim hall at the very bottom level of Greenhaven, a doorway led into a musty space. The ceiling was so low that Conor had to duck to enter. It seemed to Abeke more like a dungeon than a library.

But once they were inside, the place had a coziness to it. Rows of short bookshelves extended in every direction. They were covered in candles that flickered in the drafty chamber, dripping wax over the worn wood. The warmth of so many ruddy flames lifted some of the chill that seeped into Abeke's bones whenever she wasn't in Nilo.

"Erlan?" Meilin called out excitedly. "Are you there?"

"Meilin? Is that you?" came a gruff voice from behind one of the bookshelves.

Staring at the rows of dusty leather-bound books, they edged farther into the chamber, in a reverent hush. Until, that is, Rollan promptly bashed his head on an iron chandelier, which in turn swung right into a bookcase, rocking it backward. Dusty parchment flew everywhere.

"Careful, careful!" came the gruff voice.

A tiny Niloan man came into view around one of the shelves, wearing a sea-foam-colored robe with white fur trim that merged seamlessly with his voluminous white beard.

"Hello, Erlan!" Meilin said, giving the librarian a kiss on the cheek.

"Meilin!" Erlan said, delighted.

As the librarian walked toward them, Abeke became confused: For every step the small man took forward, there was a pattering of footfalls.

She saw the reason soon enough, when Erlan stepped to one side and revealed a large tortoise, its gray-blue scales the same hue as the librarian's robe. The tortoise blinked its rheumy eyes at them and yawned.

"It's so lovely to see you again, Meilin. I have the new edition of Shei-Lon's *Ars Geometrica*. You'll adore it. I'm still more partial to the Niloan edition, but that could just be because that's what *I* grew up reading. In any case, you won't believe the diagrams; they're woodcut prints, and simply gorgeous. Now, where is it?"

Erlan turned in a broad circle, searching for the book. His robe dragged against another shelf, sweeping a stack of books to the ground and spraying candlewax over the friends. Abeke and Conor followed after him, picking up the books and placing them back on the shelf as close as they could to their original order while Rollan stamped out the flaming wicks.

"I'd love to look at that book soon, but not today, Erlan," Meilin said. "We're here on urgent business."

"Learning is always important business," Erlan muttered. He kept rummaging around the shelves until the tortoise pointedly walked into the librarian's legs to get his attention. Erlan looked down at his spirit animal, then at Meilin, and smoothed his white hair. "Sorry. Right. Urgent business, you said?"

"Yes," Rollan said, rubbing the top of his head where it had bashed the chandelier. "Headache remedies, please."

"Oh, sorry. I designed the library myself decades ago, and, well, I've never been very tall, and I suppose I forgot other people would use it, too. So let's see," Erlan said, scratching through his beard as he scanned the candlelit shelves. "Headache remedies. I'll have to see what I have. . . ."

"He was kidding," Meilin said, scowling at Rollan.

"Says you!" said Rollan, outraged.

Meilin clamped her hand over his mouth. "Erlan, we're looking for any reference to a doorway that looks like an open jaw."

He rubbed his palms together. "That's not something you hear every day."

"Like this one," Conor said helpfully, unrolling Kovo's parchment and showing it to Erlan.

The old man squinted at the charcoal sketch. "Who drew this? It's quite good, really. Exquisite use of crosshatch shading."

"Kovo did," Conor said. "He's been drawing it repeatedly. He's obsessed with it, apparently."

Erlan instinctively recoiled. "Well, well. All the literature does point to Kovo being very smart. That was never in question." Erlan scrutinized the drawing. "Now. What is he trying to tell us?"

After a few moments, the old man sighed. "I suppose there's only one place for it. . . ."

Groaning, he padded toward a candle-covered bookshelf that was already wobbling long before the librarian drew near. Abeke braced herself to leap to the rescue, but Erlan turned before ever reaching the shelf. Instead, he faced a small stretch of blank wall nestled between all the books.

Except it wasn't a wall.

The elder Greencloak lifted a trembling hand and ran it over the bricks, finally coming to rest on one that was slightly darker than the rest. When he pressed it, ancient stones grumbled and hissed as they shifted deep in the walls, and then the bricks pivoted back, revealing a hidden room.

So many kinds of doors, Abeke thought again.

"Erlan?" Meilin said uncertainly. "You never told me there was another room here."

"No, I didn't," the librarian said wearily. "I couldn't tell anyone, not even you, Meilin. The Greencloaks have many fine qualities, but there are stories that they'd prefer to forget."

Erlan disappeared into the room, sending a breeze of cold, stale air back out in his place. Abeke shivered.

"Much of the history of the Lost Lands is contained in here," Erlan called out. "After the First Devourer War, the nation of Stetriol became a forbidden place, and knowledge of it was erased. It has taken me many, *many* years to assemble these manuscripts. Use what you discover here to help Erdas, but I'd ask you not to spread word of this collection further than you must. Not everyone would be happy to know I've been accumulating this information."

A cough, a wheeze, a puff of breath. Dust plumed out of the doorway. From within its shell, the tortoise sneezed.

"But some of these histories are older even than the Lost Lands," Erlan said, emerging from the passage with a tome bound in cracked black snakeskin. He hobbled to a broad table and laid the great book down with care. There, raised beneath the cover, was the shape of a gorilla standing on all fours.

"Kovo," Conor whispered.

"What is this book, Erlan?" Meilin asked, mistrust lacing her voice.

"I have no idea," the librarian said wistfully. "Can't read a word of it. Perhaps to keep its contents secret, it was written in a forgotten tongue—or a code. I've lost many nights trying to decipher it. But thankfully, the author was also a skilled artist." Erlan gently cracked open the cover of the book, turning each page with delicate precision.

"Here we are," he said. As he turned the next page, the air in the cramped library seemed to still.

Despite herself, Abeke gasped. There, sketched onto the page in a delicate hand, was the exact door Kovo had drawn, waiting within a set of ragged jaws. It even had the strange spiral symbol.

Rollan whistled. "Well, isn't that weird?"

Erlan grunted in agreement as he turned the next page. It was a map. A twisted ring of mountains curled into itself, dropping into a cone at the center, like the trap of an antlion. In the center of the ring, the spiral was drawn again into a stretch of mountainside surrounded by forest and ruined walls. This time the spiral was a deep crimson color. Abeke hoped it was just red ink.

"What is this place?" Meilin asked.

"The Petral Mountains, on the border between Eura and Zhong," Erlan said quietly. "A very secluded stretch. No humans have lived there for quite a while."

"This is all fine and moody," Rollan said, "but we still don't know that it's connected to what's happening with the Evertree. Kovo has tricked us before."

"Kovo is not to be trusted," Erlan said. "But in this case, I believe that the door *is* indeed connected to the Evertree."

"Why's that?" Abeke asked.

"I haven't shown you the back cover yet." Erlan closed the tome and carefully flipped it over.

There, raised beneath the snakeskin, was the outline of an enormous tree. But the tree was only half of the picture. A thin line bisected the image where the roots of the tree met the ground. Below the line, the roots spread out into a web of branches, as wide and tangled as the tree itself. Bundled deep within the roots, like an egg within a nest, was the familiar spiral.

"That's why Lenori couldn't find anything wrong with the Evertree at first," Abeke said. "She was looking outside, but the trouble is coming from *below*."

"So we have to go below, too," Conor said. "And we have to start in the Petral Mountains."

Now that Conor had said it aloud, the idea of journeying deep under the earth felt terrifying. They stared at each other in the candlelit gloom of the basement library. Abeke saw Rollan rub his head absently where he'd struck the chandelier. How far down did the Evertree go? If this library felt low and oppressive, what would it feel like to be miles underground? She couldn't speak for the others, but she knew it was nowhere she'd want to be.

Erlan clapped his hands cheerfully, cutting the sudden gloom. "Glad to be of service!"

"Good thing I didn't unpack yet," Meilin said as the old man shuffled away. "We'll leave as soon as we can. It's too bad—after that sea voyage, I'd have loved a few nights in a soft bed."

Conor shook his head and tugged unconsciously at his sleeve.

Meilin glanced from him to Abeke with questioning eyes. All Abeke could do was shrug. It wasn't her news to tell.

"Before we make any decisions, I have something to show you," Conor said miserably. "But let's go back up to the courtyard. We'll all feel better out in the daylight."

But the daylight was nearly gone. Afternoon was rapidly declining into twilight when they returned to the courtyard, the shadows lengthening and joining as they deepened toward night.

Conor had been silent all the way out to the courtyard, and now in the waning evening light he held up a hand to stop his companions. "Takoda?" he called softly. "Would you come over here? I need your help—I don't want to get any part of this story wrong."

Takoda stood up, hands clasped within his stiff blue robe.

When the boy stepped away, Kovo startled and grunted loudly, making a flurry of signs. Takoda waited for him to finish, then made a simple sign back and pointed to Abeke and the others.

Kovo signed more and more emphatically, baring his teeth. Abeke felt her hands tighten into fists. Would Kovo attack Takoda, even though they were bonded?

Calmly, Takoda repeated the same simple sign and pointed at the group.

All was still for a moment, then Kovo strained against his chain and roared right into Takoda's face, the noise echoing across the bare courtyard. Chest heaving in anger, Kovo grunted and hurled himself heavily onto the flagstones, his back to them. He punched the ground once, and Abeke heard a crack where the sturdy flagstone split in two.

Visibly shaken, Takoda crossed over. "I think he's . . . concerned that you won't heed his warning. Sorry."

"Are you okay?" Abeke asked.

Takoda nodded, lips sealed in a straight line. "What do you need from me?"

Conor had clenched his jaw so tightly that it was shaking. Abeke put a reassuring hand on her friend's wrist, and was relieved when he let it stay.

"When we went to get Kovo and Takoda, Zerif attacked," Conor began. "He was . . . different, somehow. More intense. And here was the strangest thing: He had that spiral symbol on his forehead." Conor swallowed. "While we were driving him back, Zerif uncorked a small black bottle. I managed to grab it from his hand." Conor breathed out softly.

From the center of the courtyard, Kovo turned his head enough so he could stare at them, his scarlet eyes narrowed.

"What was in the bottle?" Meilin asked.

"It was . . ." Conor faltered.

Takoda spoke gently, answering for him. "It was alive. Some kind of worm."

Conor nodded, casting a grateful look at Takoda. "I chopped at it as soon as it crawled out of the bottle. I thought it was dead, but a little chunk of it wriggled up my blade and entered a cut on my wrist. And that piece . . ."

Gritting his teeth, Conor rolled up his sleeve.

Though she'd already heard the story, this was the first time Abeke had seen Conor's wound. She gasped. Starting at a red scab at Conor's wrist, a tendril of gray passed up his forearm, ending slightly before his elbow. It paralleled a blue vein in the middle of Conor's arm. But while the vein was still, this tendril quivered like something alive, just below the skin.

At the elbow, where the living tendril ended, the knob of it throbbed and shifted, curling into new versions of the same shape.

A spiral.

A DESPERATE PLAN

Revealing the parasite went just as Conor feared it would. Abeke gasped and turned her head away; Rollan cast his eyes to the ground; Meilin gritted her teeth and forced herself to keep looking despite her obvious disgust. Conor watched all of it, his heart twisting. There was something bitterly wrong with him, and now he was going to lose the people he loved most in the world because of it.

Conor pulled his sleeve down low so it covered the creature. The creature *inside of him.* "I don't know what it is," he said. "It's been moving ever since it entered me. I can barely sleep."

Takoda looked at him with deep pity, and Conor hated it. He felt his face twist into a humiliated scowl. His heart was racing so much, he wondered if his friends could see his veins thudding violently under his skin.

"Hey," Rollan said, wrapping his arm around Conor's shoulders. "We're going to figure this out. You know that, right?"

There was tension in Rollan's voice. He was lying. Conor was sure of it.

"Does it hurt?" asked Meilin.

Conor shrugged Rollan's arm off his shoulder. "Not too much. Sometimes I think if I ignored it, it might go away. It's just so . . . disgusting."

Rollan wouldn't give up. He threw his arms around his friend. "You've been disgusting ever since we've known you."

Conor's heart filled with relief. Who knew it could feel so good to be teased? But Rollan had always been an expert at it, making him feel loved even as he took him down.

Finally Conor could voice what was worrying him most: "Even though only a small piece of it got inside me, this thing is working its way up my arm. Zerif's was in his forehead. I think that's where it's heading." Conor's stomach lurched. "What happens when it gets there?"

"It's not possible for you to become like Zerif," Rollan said flatly. "He's got better hair, for starters."

"I feel like cutting it out," Conor said.

"Absolutely not," Meilin said. "No way are you cutting into your arm."

"You said even that little fragment of the parasite was able to infect you," Abeke said. "Last thing we want to do is risk splitting it into more pieces."

Conor shuddered, then reluctantly nodded.

"All of Greenhaven's most capable healers have gone to help the Evertree," Abeke continued. "Who's left?"

"The best healer of them all, that's who," Meilin said. "Jhi."

The next dawn, the friends met for an early breakfast in the Greenhaven dining room, slate-colored rain drumming the stained-glass windows. The night before, they'd marked in ink how far up Conor's arm the creature had reached. This morning it was only a tiny bit farther.

"It's slowed," Conor said, sighing. "At least there's that."

Meilin had spent the night on the floor of Conor's room so Jhi could be near him while he slept. The panda had worked her healing throughout the night, and though there had been benefits, they'd clearly been minimal. "Did anyone get any sleep?" Meilin asked.

Her friends stared back at her balefully.

Meilin's hair was sticking straight up in the back. Rollan cut a glance at Conor, silently daring him to comment on it. Abeke gave them a severe look: *Don't you dare.*

"While I was staring at the moonbeams on Conor's ceiling," Meilin continued, "here's what I figured: We have two problems to deal with. Zerif is out collecting the Great Beasts as they appear. And something—probably related—is poisoning the Evertree from below."

"Lenori will know where the Great Beasts are going to appear shortly before it happens," Abeke said. "We could try to intercept Zerif next time, and stop him for good."

"Regardless, someone should check out this mysterious door and figure out what's poisoning the Evertree," Meilin said. "Problem is, we can't all do both at once."

Abeke nodded. "We'll have to split up."

"Okay," Rollan said, gritting his teeth. "I don't like it, but it's not like we haven't done this before. We'll be back together before long."

Conor watched as Meilin fixed Rollan a complicated, mournful look.

"What?" Rollan asked. "What did I say?"

Meilin switched to a stop-being-such-a-dolt look. "I'll need to stay with Conor . . . so Jhi can heal him as much as she can."

"So? . . . Oh."

"Conor and I can check out the door," Meilin said solemnly. "Rollan and Abeke are our best trackers, which means you two should find the other Great Beasts."

"I could go alone," Abeke offered.

"Absolutely not," Rollan said, sighing. "Zerif was dangerous *before* he had a bunch of Great Beasts as his personal bodyguards."

"Thank you," Abeke said, sighing with relief. "I'd argue harder, but I have to admit the idea was terrifying."

Conor wasn't eager to follow the strange doorway into whatever darkness lay beyond it, but he couldn't see any better option. He was terrified by the worm living inside him. What if Zerif could use it against him somehow—or against his friends?

Meilin and Rollan were staring at each other with moony longing, but Abeke looked right into Conor's eyes. He could tell from her expression that she'd followed everything that had just passed through his mind. She lay a hand on her friend's infected wrist. With one move she'd told him that she wasn't scared of his sickness. Conor's eyes stung with gratitude.

"I'll probably regret suggesting this," Meilin said, "but Kovo is the key to that door, which means he and Takoda should come with us when we go check it out."

"*And* a full detail of Greencloaks," Abeke added. "You'll need whatever we can spare to watch him."

"So we won't have Kovo's sparkling conversation to entertain us here in Greenhaven?" Rollan asked. "That's really such a shame."

Abeke frowned. "Investigate the door, guys. See if it's safe. But remember that you don't have to do anything more than that: If that entrance is as old as we think, any tunnels beneath it may have collapsed already. Don't get yourselves trapped."

"With the worst enemy we've ever known, no less," Conor said.

"We'll be careful," Meilin said, casting one last long look at Rollan. "And we'll be back before you know it."

THE PETRAL MOUNTAINS

Takoda was falling behind.

The monastery in Nilo had been so tranquil. The quiet, meditative men and women who had taken him in spent their days shuffling through terra-cotta hallways, whispering to one another in deliberative tones or meditating in the study.

Takoda had spent his life in sandals, and now he was wearing a pair of heavy boots he'd borrowed from Conor. He struggled to keep up. His life had changed so much, so rapidly. He'd left Nilo for the first time, traveled over the sea to Greenhaven, and now he was in the Petral foothills. The monks who raised him were so very far away. A lush green cloak hung around his shoulders. Takoda stroked it admiringly as they trekked.

Meilin was watching. "Remember that you're just wearing a green cloak," she said, a touch imperiously. "That's different from *being* a Greencloak."

Takoda grimaced and continued marching. Sure, he hadn't joined the order or anything, but all the same he enjoyed the feeling of the heavy cloak clasped around his narrow shoulders. He probably wouldn't say no if they asked him to be a Greencloak someday.

As if he had sensed Takoda's thoughts, Kovo grunted in irritation. Takoda realized he'd pulled a few paces ahead, and returned to the ape's side. Kovo never liked it when Takoda strayed, but the boy wasn't naive enough to think Kovo missed him.

The Greencloak delegation kept itself in a tight circle around Kovo. At first it had made Takoda nervous, but that soon turned to relief when he realized it meant *he* wouldn't be responsible for the gorilla.

Once a spirit animal bond grew strong, sometimes the animal could disappear as a tattoo somewhere on its human partner's body. The decision to use passive form was ultimately the animal's, however, and Kovo clearly was nowhere near trusting Takoda. So the smiths at Greenhaven had fashioned Kovo a collar with two rings that attached to long poles. Two Greencloaks took up those poles now, positioned on either side of him.

Kovo suffered his indignity stoically, keeping his true feelings well hidden. The powerful gorilla clambered easily over the ground, knuckle-walking his way through brambles and thickets while the Greencloaks struggled to keep pace. As often as not Kovo had his gaze focused up in the clouds; Takoda frequently found himself following Kovo's eyes and wondering what he saw up there.

When they took their first break for the day, Kovo

basked in the chill sunshine with his eyes closed, face to the breeze with a serene expression. Long before his captivity in Greenhaven's courtyard, Kovo had been imprisoned for centuries for his crimes. Even chained to two poles, he must be finding this relative freedom sweet.

The Petral foothills were like nothing Takoda had ever seen in Nilo. Brisk winds sheared off jagged, low mountains, sending waves of sharp chill down through the desperate leaves clinging to scrabbly bushes. The soil was thin and pebbly, dotted with broad flat stones barbed in green moss. The whole region was one giant shallow basin; ever since they'd crested the mountains at the Eura-Zhong border, they'd been slowly descending—toward what, Takoda didn't know.

He planted his numb, red fingers under his arms to keep them at least a little warm.

"How is Olvan so fast?" Takoda asked Meilin, huffing as he struggled to make his way up a rise. His breath made little cotton puffs wherever he went. The leader of the Greencloaks was bounding over a rise half a mile ahead.

Meilin shrugged. "His spirit animal is a moose. I guess we're in a moose-y kind of place."

Meilin had brought Jhi into passive state, to spare the panda the trek. It was a moment that would forever be seared in Takoda's memory: As soon as the ground grew rough, Meilin had taken Jhi's face in her hands and they took a good long look at each other, both of them nodding once they'd finished their wordless deliberation. Takoda couldn't imagine a spirit animal relationship more different from his own.

"Briggan is a wolf," Conor said. "But even he's finding it hard to keep up." Beside him, Briggan barked indignantly at the challenge. The wolf took off hurtling over the countryside, soon overpassing even Olvan. He took occasional leaps of pure joy.

Conor grinned after him, the worry so frequently on his face melting momentarily away.

Toward late morning, Olvan called the group to a halt on a rocky crest. "Look!" he called triumphantly.

Takoda scanned the landscape but could see nothing all that different from the rest of the steppe they'd traveled. "It's . . . pretty?" he tried.

"Olvan, I see what you mean," Conor said. "It's just like the map!"

Now that Conor had pointed it out, Takoda could see it. At the lowest point in the valley, dense shrubbery closed in, masking whatever was at the bottom.

He heard a scuffle behind him, and his heart seized when he turned and saw the two Greencloaks, both barrel-chested Eurans, struggling mightily to keep Kovo in line with the collar. Kovo kept walking forward, despite his restraints. Then, with no apparent effort at all, he took a leap, yanking the poles clean out of the guards' hands.

No! Be good! Takoda signed.

Kovo stared back, expressionless. It was typical; sometimes Kovo would sign fluently at Takoda, and other times he'd pretend not to understand a single gesture. The message he sent by being so selective was unmistakably clear: *I'm the one in charge. Don't forget it.*

Conor fell into a fighting position, but Takoda laid a restraining hand on his new friend's shoulder. He wouldn't stop the Greencloaks from battling Kovo if it came to blows, but Takoda knew his spirit animal well enough to see that the ape wasn't about to attack. There was the trace of a wicked smile on his face, though—clearly Kovo had enjoyed the game of pretending that he was under their control . . . and had enjoyed proving it wrong even more.

Kovo stood on all fours at the top of the ridge, scrutinizing the densely wooded basin. Olvan edged close to the ape, his moose hovering over him protectively. A shiver passed over Takoda as he watched his spirit animal—the Great Beast that had nearly conquered the world—stand shoulder-to-shoulder with the leader of the Greencloaks. With that one simple display of force, Kovo had made it hard to say who was truly in charge.

The two burly Greencloaks brought Kovo's poles back up, but the ape took advantage of the pause to barrel forward, dragging one of the men a dozen feet before the surprised Euran let go.

"Briggan, tail him!" Conor said. But the wolf was already on it. Nose low to the ground and tail pointed straight back, he shot off on the chase, his whole body taking the shape of a javelin. Conor, Meilin, and Takoda fell in behind, scrambling to keep their footing on the dim and scrabbly forest trail. Takoda heard Conor tumble beside him, but couldn't afford the time to help him up—

Briggan was letting out a stream of barks so that the rest could more easily follow, but they were getting fainter as he and the ape pulled ahead.

When Conor and Takoda flagged, Meilin assuredly sprinted past, easily hurdling upturned roots and fallen trees. Takoda picked up speed as he switched from following Briggan's sounds to watching Meilin's whipping hair as she leaped and ran.

Though he couldn't risk letting his gaze leave the path for even a second, Takoda became aware of ruined walls blurring by. Beneath his feet, the ground changed from soil and moss to overgrown mosaic floors and shards of dull broken pottery. "We've entered some ancient city," Takoda puffed to Conor. "Abandoned."

"Maybe we're about to find out why!" Meilin shouted from up ahead.

"Be careful," Takoda called. "Don't trust Kovo!"

"Don't you worry about that!" Meilin disappeared around a curve, then yelled back for Takoda and Conor to stop. Takoda was already barreling around the mossy brick corner, though, and nearly slammed into her. She threw her arms around him to bring him to a halt before he tumbled.

As Takoda caught his breath, he realized they were standing at the edge of what might have been a moat during a rainier season. It was only about four feet deep but a good dozen feet across, its bottom full of pine needles and dirt. It extended far into the distance on one side and stopped in a solid rock wall on the other; they'd have to cross it to continue the trail.

Kovo must have made the same decision for himself: He was already standing on the debris clogging the moat, raised on two legs as he stared apprehensively along its length. The gorilla was perfectly motionless, and Takoda could see the tension rippling up and down his muscular legs. Clearly Kovo's footing was precarious beneath the dirt and pine needles, though Takoda couldn't see exactly why.

Stop. Return, Takoda signed.

Kovo roared and made one simple sign, his scarlet eyes glittering in anger. *No.*

"Look!" Conor said, pointing at the cluttered moat floor.

At first Takoda couldn't see what Conor was referring to. Then, glinting from below, he saw rusty spear tips where the leaves and rubble parted a far ways down. It was a trap! But the rigged pit must have been so old that it was clogged, and hadn't fired. Yet.

Stop. Return, Takoda signed again. He cursed. If only he and Kovo knew more than ten symbols, he could explain the danger.

But Kovo had already figured it out. His gaze returned to the terrain below and the stones that shifted precariously under his feet. He must have raced over the moat, and then gone still once he sensed the danger below.

But not still enough.

Kovo's weight shifted slightly, and Takoda heard a grinding sound deep underground as a mechanism started moving. Kovo flashed a desperate look at Takoda. The grinding sound intensified, and then the stones under Kovo's feet gave way. Kovo cried out and suddenly dropped, disappearing up to his waist in stones and soil.

If he'd had a moment to think, Takoda might have let Kovo continue to fall. But he saw the ape tumbling to his death, and instinct took over. Takoda dashed toward his spirit animal, over the wobbling stones of the pit floor, which fell toward the spikes with every step.

A furious light burned in Kovo's eyes, and then, in a flash, his arm was around Takoda's waist. Leaping into the air, the gorilla just managed to catch the far wall of the moat and hurl himself up. The ground beneath the moat roiled, then disappeared as rocks and debris tumbled somewhere below.

Takoda fell against Kovo, landing hard onto the ape's chest. For a moment the two remained there in a strange embrace, struggling to catch their breath. Then Kovo pushed Takoda roughly to one side and rose on all fours.

"Are you okay, Takoda?" Meilin called.

He couldn't seem to get enough breath in his lungs to reply. But he nodded as the stones in the pit continued to gnash and fall away.

"What do we do?" Conor asked Meilin. To Briggan, though, the right way forward was obvious. The wolf backed up, got a running start, and leaped across the churning stones of the moat.

"Go!" Conor cried to Meilin, after seeing Briggan scrabble up to safety on the far side of the shifting floor.

Briggan had apparently had enough of Kovo's chase. The wolf's hackles raised and he took feinting lunges toward the ape, long teeth bared and growls rumbling out from deep in his throat.

Kovo and Briggan would have to fight it out themselves. Takoda's attention was on the far side of the moat, where great gaps now appeared, revealing even more spikes. For a few moments, at least, there was still enough earth intact that his Greencloak friends might be able to pick their way across.

Meilin jumped first, aiming for the most solid section of the moat floor. She landed, but sank up to her ankles in the loose soil. It held long enough for her to leap to the next. With each hop she left fewer footing options open to Conor.

Takoda watched as the pale boy gritted his teeth and chose his own path, a few feet to one side of Meilin. Looking at the pit of rusty spears below, Takoda's mind filled with flashing horror.

Meilin grunted as she made her final leap, only just reaching the far side. Her fingers clawed deep into rocky dirt. "Come on, Conor!" she cried.

Conor was perched on a teetering square of earth. There was only one foothold left that he could hop to in order to reach the far side, but it was already crumbling. He paused, unsure of himself, unsure of whether it would hold. Then, before Conor could act, the ground beneath him gave way and he was falling toward rusty spear points—

—until a strong arm reached out from the far side of the moat and snagged the belt around Conor's midsection. Takoda watched in disbelief as, with impossible agility, Kovo stepped right around Briggan's snapping jaws, reached to fish out Conor, and hurled the boy through the air. Conor skidded along the ground and got to his feet as soon as he could, looking back to see Kovo climbing out of the half-fallen moat. The ape raised himself onto all fours, panting heavily. Briggan had ceased his attack and looked completely puzzled, his hackles still raised and one hesitant paw in the air.

"What just happened?" Conor asked, shaking his head as he staggered to his feet.

"Kovo saved your life," Takoda said, kneeling beside the gorilla. Kovo stared furiously at his hands, clenched into tight fists in his lap. He raised one and used it to shove Takoda away.

"It wasn't a moat," Meilin said, peering down. "It was a trap. Whoever's city this once was, they didn't want anyone going farther."

Takoda ignored her. *Thank you*, he signed to Kovo.

The ape didn't make any response. He'd never made the signs for *you're welcome*—or *thank you* or *sorry*, for that matter—to Takoda. Maybe he hadn't learned them. Maybe he didn't know the concepts.

The ape stared at Takoda, red eyes glittering. Takoda signed one more time. *Thank you.*

Kovo grunted. Then he sprang into motion, hurtling past Briggan and hustling off down the trail. A second too late, Briggan lunged at him, his jaws clamping over empty air. Briggan shook his head, surprised to have missed, then took off to follow Kovo, his teeth bared.

"Do you have any idea where Kovo is going?" Conor asked Takoda.

Takoda shook his head. "I wish I did. Kovo only signs to me when it's useful for him."

"Hustle, guys. We don't want to lose them," Meilin said. She took off after Briggan and Kovo.

"What about Olvan and the others?" Conor asked, casting a glance back along the trail. They could hear the sounds of the rest of the Greencloaks, still far off.

"They'll have to go around or find some other way across," Meilin said, "Kovo can't go free. That has to be our first priority."

Part of Takoda thought that losing Kovo sounded pretty appealing, actually. But he suspected that, for good or bad, he'd always have Kovo to deal with.

Takoda saw Briggan's tail only a short ways down the path, fur sticking out stiffly. He couldn't see what the wolf was looking at, but he was at full attention.

"What is it, Briggan?" Conor asked.

As they turned the corner, Takoda saw it.

The giant maw.

It was like the earth itself had a mouth, open and hungry, waiting for prey to fall in. Cupped in the face of a mossy shale cliff side, here were the rows of sharp teeth above and below. And above it all, carved into the cave's overhang, the symbol of a twisting spiral.

It looked like that mouth wanted to drink the world above, drink and drink, as long as it took to swallow the sky down.

Seeing the gaping maw, all Takoda wanted to do was turn around and go back. Rattled, he tried to reason with himself. *This cave entrance must have been designed* to strike terror, he scolded himself, *and you're letting it work.*

Kovo was on his feet, swaying trancelike as he stared into the opening. Then he got down to all fours and stepped forward.

"Can you get him to stop?" Conor asked Takoda. "Olvan and the others should be here for this."

"Um, no," Takoda said. "But if you want to try, be my guest."

Kovo stepped under the overhang, then disappeared into the darkness.

"He can't get away!" Meilin gasped. "Kovo has a plan, and whatever it is, I don't trust it!"

Briggan looked at Conor, waiting for him to act. But Conor was retreating inside himself, his hand nervously clutching the arm where the parasite was growing and spreading. Seeing Conor's indecision, Briggan barked.

"This is what we came here for, right?" Takoda said, lips set in a grim line. "Saving the Evertree. I'm going after him."

Steeling his courage, he stepped over the carved lower teeth and entered the gaping jaw. He could hear the others following behind him. Whether or not Takoda trusted Kovo, they were all going to follow the ape. The fate of the Evertree—of the spirit animal bond itself—depended on them.

Light had been scarce in the dense forest city, but it was pitch-dark beneath the overhang. Takoda reached at his belt for one of the skinny torches Conor had given him from the Greenhaven stock, and struck it against the attached flint. It lit with a flurry of sparks and then a steady flame.

Takoda gasped. Scarlet eyes glittered at him, only inches away. Takoda nearly dropped the torch in fright. Steadying himself, drawing on every ounce of self-control the monks had instilled in him, Takoda forced himself to meet Kovo's gaze. The gorilla gave one grunt in his direction and made a sign: *Follow*. Then he lumbered off, his black hair soon merging with the surrounding darkness.

Meilin and Conor tight by his side, Takoda shuffled after Kovo, probing the ground with the toe of his boot to make sure they didn't walk into another chasm.

Briggan whined softly but kept moving forward. The wolf had better dark vision than the humans did, so it was a small reassurance that he was comfortable with traveling deeper into the cave.

Takoda felt a sudden cold draft, then the ground pitched unexpectedly downward. He swung the torch forward, and its light caught the trail of silver hair along Kovo's spine. The gorilla was close in front of them, staring at something farther along the passageway.

Takoda maneuvered the torch so it would illuminate whatever had caught the ape's attention.

The stone walls of the cave dead-ended at an ancient wooden door. The wood was splintered and riddled with wormholes, and probably would have fallen apart centuries ago if it hadn't been for the thick rusty bands that reinforced it lengthwise and crossways.

"Here's our doorway," breathed Meilin.

"Olvan!" Conor yelled, in the blind hope that the elder

Greencloak had somehow found a way to follow. The only response was his own echo. They were on their own.

"Well, we'll just have to wait here," Meilin said. "No way we're going through that door without the others."

"That sounds wise," Takoda said, though he didn't relish the idea of waiting in this dark and mysterious cave, either. He could hear large skittering insects somewhere nearby, and the plunk-plunk of dripping water beneath the hissing of his torch.

"We should go back into the daylight and wait for them," Conor said.

Apparently Kovo didn't relish waiting by the door, either. But his solution was different: The gorilla picked up its iron-ring handle and, before anyone could stop him, gave it a tug.

The door held firm. Briggan growled warningly, snapping his jaws.

"Stop him!" Conor said.

Meilin was the first to leap to the attack, her quarterstaff out. She streaked it toward Kovo's head, but he pivoted and knocked it aside with a massive forearm. The quarterstaff glanced away harmlessly.

The gorilla gave the door another mighty tug.

It was Briggan's turn to attack. The wolf lunged forward and caught Kovo's ankle in his jaws. Kovo roared in pain but kept his footing.

Enraged, Kovo switched tactics. Instead of pulling, he battered.

Yanking his ankle out of the wolf's jaws, the gorilla took two thudding steps before hitting the door squarely with his meaty shoulder, the poles that had once restrained him clattering at his sides. The door bent and groaned, then finally tumbled from its hinges entirely.

There was a rush of fetid air from a frigid black corridor, and an ominous rumble.

Kovo stepped in.

As soon as he did, there was a crunching sound. The heavy stone arch above the door fell an inch. The rocks shivered: They wouldn't hold for long.

Takoda wavered. From behind him, the crunching sound got louder. It sounded like loud crackling now, almost like a giant tree being felled. He could flee back into the daylight if he wanted.

Meilin yelled, but her words were lost in the clamor.

The stone around them crackled again, a sound almost like fireworks, and then it roared. Suddenly Briggan was rushing by Takoda, sprinting into the corridor after Kovo. The kids ran after the wolf, hurtling into the passage just as the cave behind them collapsed in on itself. That door must have been holding up the great weight of stone and earth, and once it had fallen, all the rest had tumbled in, too.

"Run!" Meilin yelled, her footsteps clattering in the darkness.

Something heavy caught Takoda's heel and he spilled, tumbling onto slick stone. The corridor slanted sharply down, and as he rolled forward he bowled into someone—Meilin or Conor—and they tumbled together. Down became up, then went back to being down. Takoda's nose smashed into a wall. He tasted blood in his mouth as he continued to plummet deep into the earth, only slowly coming to rest.

For a moment, all was noise. Then black stillness. Though he couldn't see any of it, rock dust must have been everywhere—every time Takoda breathed in, he coughed and gagged.

Takoda felt Briggan's tongue lick his cheek. He managed to free one hand where it was wrenched under him, and reached up to stroke the side of the wolf's snout. If Briggan was safe, did that mean the others were? The thought gave him some strength, which he used to lift his head and look around.

On his other side he discovered that the torch was still lit, sputtering against the stone nearby. Takoda took it into his sore fingers and lifted it.

Meilin and Conor were sprawled together on the other side of Briggan, laid out flat. Takoda watched them blink back at him in the darkness. "Are you okay?" he asked.

"Yes," Meilin groaned. "Just."

Conor nodded gingerly.

Takoda didn't need to ask Kovo whether he was okay. The ape was seated to one side. His black hair was covered in a soft layer of clay dust, but otherwise he seemed unaffected by the collapse. For a moment his penetrating eyes seemed to look right through Takoda. Then he turned his head and peered off into the darkness, where a corridor sloped into the void, seemingly without end.

Calmly, as easily as if it had been made of wet paper, Kovo reached up and plucked off his collar.

HUNTING

"**B**UT IT'S SO *CLOSE*," ROLLAN SAID, AN UNCHARACTERISTIC whine to his voice as they sailed past the Concorba skyline. He stretched his arms as far as he could over the railing of *Tellun's Pride II*, as if hoping to stroke the buildings.

Their ship was going right by the city where Rollan had spent his childhood. Since he'd been a homeless thief back then, Abeke hadn't expected to see Rollan feeling nostalgic for the place. But home was always home, she knew, and that fact could never be changed.

"Don't worry, we'll visit Concorba on the way back," she said. "You can give me a tour, and we'll stop in and say hello to all the shop owners you stole from back in the day. That should be fun."

Rollan chuckled, but it didn't last long. Abeke noticed his hand absently toying with his green cloak. Maybe Rollan actually did want to go to Concorba, wanted to let everyone from his street urchin past know how much he'd made of himself.

"Maybe on the way back we can stop in the market and see if they have anything our friends would like," Abeke continued quietly. "I'll help you pick out something for Meilin."

"She's the one who gets to go cave diving," Rollan said. "Meilin should be picking a gift out for *me*. Like a fossilized cave bat or something."

It was windy on deck, and Abeke wrapped her own cloak tightly around herself, tucking it under her arms for extra warmth. Much as she tried to stay open-minded, she suspected she was never going to like northern Amaya. The people were friendly, and there were cloudless skies and vibrant woods circling brilliant blue lakes. But it was also so *cold*. It would only get colder, too: *Tellun's Pride II* would be heading farther north into the wild lake region before they disembarked.

Rollan smiled ruefully at himself. "When Lenori sent word that another Great Beast was being reborn, I hoped she'd send us to some tropical island. Like maybe Mulop had showed up beside a pristine beach, and we could have a nice philosophical conversation with our favorite octopus while sipping from coconuts."

"Could be Ninani the Swan," Abeke mused. "Since swans spend time in the north of Amaya during the summer. It's spring now, but she might have arrived here early."

Rollan snapped his fingers. "Arax the Ram, of course! He was from Amaya."

An idea suddenly struck Abeke. "You don't think it could be . . . Tellun?" The idea of it was awe-inspiring. The other Great Beasts had often deferred to Tellun. The elk had been their leader, powerful enough to imprison even Kovo.

"Tellun," Rollan said, knocking on the wooden rail of *Tellun's Pride II*. "Huh. That would be appropriate enough, wouldn't it?"

When a cry rose from the ship's crow's nest, Abeke fell into a fighting pose and prepared to summon Uraza. But Rollan laid a restraining hand on her arm. "That means the crew sighted the drop-off point. We're nearly there."

Abeke forced her shoulders to relax. She'd been tense ever since she got on board, and because Uraza hated ship travel, she didn't even have the comfort of her leopard companion to sustain her. With its burnished cherry wood, the new flagship of the Greencloaks was even more beautiful than the previous, but this trip had brought back memories of navigating with Shane all the way to Greenhaven, sharing tender moments on deck, only to arrive and discover that he'd betrayed them all. That felt so long ago now, but as much as she tried to blot him from her mind, memories of the handsome blond boy resurfaced in unexpected moments.

The ship pulled up at a simple wooden pier that jutted from the mossy banks of the lake far into the sparkling water. This was the last spot of deep water before the inlet they were traveling on dissolved into streams and tributaries. From here they'd have to continue on foot.

Abeke and Rollan clambered below and emerged with the rucksacks they'd packed and repacked during their few days at sea, struggling on the swaying deck to get the straps over their shoulders.

"You know," Rollan said as *Tellun's Pride II* eased alongside the pier, "it might work to our advantage that we'll be hunting for our meals. Many of the people of Northern Amaya are nomadic, following the herds throughout the year. They sold meat in Concorba sometimes. Finding good hunting should also mean finding them."

Abeke's fingers strayed to the smooth Niloan wood of the short bow strapped to her back. She hadn't needed to hunt while at Greenhaven, and she missed the pleasure of it. Not the killing of the animal—that always came with a fierce sorrow—but roaming the open country, at one with the natural world.

Abeke's heavy canvas bag creaked and shifted as she stepped toward the gangplank. "We need all the luck we can get," Abeke said, "if we want to find the next Great Beast before Zerif does."

Abeke and Rollan fleetly made their way down the pier, striding out into brisk open air. Abeke opened her arms and stared up at the cloudless sky, its broad blue struck through with sunshine. She couldn't control herself—she let out a loud giggle at the beautiful and grand adventure promised by that huge sky. She practically danced off the ship.

"What's gotten into you?" Rollan chuckled. But then Essix left her perch at the summit of the ship's crow's nest and swooped over them, giving a joyful cry. Rollan, too, broke into a broad smile. When Abeke released Uraza, the leopard sprang forward, bounding over the grassy tufts that dotted the firm black soil of the Amayan earth. Abeke laughed out loud as Uraza hunted an azure butterfly, pouncing after it wherever it fled.

It felt great to be free.

"Where to?" Rollan asked.

"Anywhere!"

"No seriously, where to?"

Abeke pivoted, scanning the landscape. The land stretched flat as far as she could see, cupped on three sides by snowcapped mountains. There was a *lot* of territory to investigate. "Good question," she said, stalling.

Rollan smirked. "Erlan told us that springtime means the yak are herding and heading north. We should be able to catch them wherever we see the most green, because that's where there's food for them to eat."

Abeke gaped at him, dumbfounded.

"What?" Rollan said defensively. "I can't have a good idea every once in a while?"

"It's a great idea," Abeke said, smiling to herself. "Scouting the greenest area means first getting to a vantage point. I say we climb that hill over there and see what we can see."

"Hill?! By *hill* do you mean that staggeringly high mountain?"

Abeke grinned and started off.

Rollan grumbled all the way up, but Abeke sensed he didn't mean it. She was well aware of his sprightly step and how his eyes shone whenever he looked up at the brown arc of Essix wheeling in the bright sky. Abeke felt her body limbering during the hike, long-unused muscles stretching and lengthening.

It was late afternoon by the time they crested the summit, orange scatters of light from the declining sun bursting over the landscape. Between dense stands of pine were rolling expanses of emerald grass, and passing along one of those swaths was the largest herd of animals Abeke had ever seen. There were so many of them that at first Abeke thought she was seeing a river.

"Amayan Yak," Rollan reported. "I used to see their pelts for sale in the Concorba market, but I've never seen a live one before. Any hunter worth her salt in this region will be tailing them."

"Which means we need to be tailing them as well," Abeke said. "Though I don't think we'll be reaching that herd by sundown."

"Time to make camp," Rollan said. "And let's do it somewhere other than this windy mountaintop, please."

The next day, they made better time than Abeke had predicted; it wasn't yet midday before they'd reached the edge of the herd. A pair of elderly yaks were lagging behind, ribs stark under their patchy fur. Though either of them would make for an easy kill, Abeke resisted stringing her bow and taking one down. She and Rollan had discovered fresh water and plump breadtree buds near their campsite, and they'd filled their bellies without needing to hunt.

It became clear that Abeke had made the right choice when the pair of yaks parted and revealed a calf between them, no more than a few days old, poking its way forward on knocking knees. Perhaps its own mother had died, and this elderly pair was caring for the little beast. It, too, would make for an easy kill. Though Abeke had spared these yaks, she knew that another hunter easily might not; they'd strayed too far from the herd and were easy pickings.

Beside her, Rollan made a loud clicking noise at the back of his throat. All three yaks stilled, heads raised. From where he and Abeke were hidden in a thatch of plainsgrass, Rollan clicked again. The yaks startled and raced back toward their herd.

"What do you think you're doing?" Abeke asked.

"They need to be back with the safety of their kind," Rollan said indignantly. "I only—"

"You clearly don't know herding animals!" Abeke pointed to the herd, where the three scared yaks were joining the rest, bleating their heads off. Alarmed, the thousands of yaks took off at high speed. The resulting roar shook the countryside, the ground rumbling.

"Oh," Rollan said quietly. "I think I caused a stampede."

"Yes," Abeke sighed. "You definitely caused a stampede."

Giving up on remaining camouflage, Abeke took off sprinting toward the herd. Rollan and Uraza followed, the leopard loping quickly through the grass, soon overtaking Rollan. Her spots might not blend in with this northern environment, but Uraza could still move more quietly than any other creature Abeke had ever known. Though the yaks were fast, between Uraza on the ground and Essix soaring overhead, they'd have no trouble locating the herd once it calmed down.

After half an hour of tracking, they came to a bottleneck

where the forest closed in on either side, choking the plains tight. The herd had to slow as it passed through. "Let's keep ourselves a few hundred paces behind," Abeke called. "Don't forget our goal is to find whoever's hunting this herd, not to stress the animals."

Rollan nodded and slowed. "We could use a break anyway," he panted. Uraza stared at him—a little disdainfully, Abeke thought—and then returned her alert gaze to the herd as it pulled ahead. Abeke gave the frustrated leopard a comforting pet on the flank.

The herd slowed even more, and Abeke and Rollan fell farther and farther behind to wait it out. Once the yaks were clear of the trees, the friends could finally continue forward. The woods edged in as they passed through the bottleneck—the narrowest point was only a few paces away. Abeke peered in curiously as she passed but could see nothing moving.

The same wasn't true for the other side, though. Abeke heard a yowl behind her and turned just in time to see a mountain lion launch out of the woods at her, claws outstretched and ready to rend her apart.

Caught by surprise, Abeke gasped and stumbled.

The tawny, muscular cat hadn't counted on Uraza, though. The leopard was instantly on the attack, leaping so her own body impacted the mountain lion's before it could strike Abeke. The two cats tumbled in the dirt, rolling until they crashed into the side of a boulder.

It was a close match. Uraza was longer, but this cat was more muscular. It gashed the leopard with its powerful back claws, and Uraza howled in pain.

Abeke immediately had her bow off her back and struggled to get it strung, cursing herself for not having predicted an ambush. Rollan's dagger needed no preparations, though, Abeke saw from the corner of her eye as he ran toward the cats. Essix shrieked in the air, probably set to dive in and join the combat.

They would have had this under control. If the mountain lion had been alone.

Abeke felt a sharp pain in her spine, and suddenly her body no longer obeyed her commands. She dropped slackly to the earth, the agony in the back of her neck eclipsing all else. Though she couldn't see what it was, there was a vise on her spine, pushing ever tighter, and she felt a hot line of blood—her blood—stream down her face as she lay still. *My spine*, she thought. *Something is trying to crush my spine.*

Then there was a rush of air, and a falcon's scream sounded in her ear. The vise on her neck lifted, and Abeke was able to get her arms under herself enough to see Essix rolling with a second mountain lion. Brown and white feathers flurried into the air.

The element of surprise had allowed Essix to get the mountain lion off Abeke, but the falcon stood no chance in an open combat against a ferocious cat. Fortunately, Rollan was soon upon them. He struck wildly with his dagger, opening a gash along the mountain lion's midsection. Howling, the cat disengaged from Essix and limped away. The falcon hopped into the air but flopped back to ground, one wing dragging, clearly wounded.

The first mountain lion had wriggled free of Uraza and the two faced off against each other, circling in the dirt while they made low growls, fangs bared. As the second lion limped off after the departing yak herd, though, the first one broke away and followed.

Rollan was immediately upon Essix, murmuring words of concern, his arms around the wounded bird. While Essix held her beak closed, stoically silent, Rollan gently probed her wing. "I don't think it's broken," he said, relieved. "Just strained."

Uraza came over and tenderly nudged Essix's wingtip with her nose, making soft concerned meows. Then the leopard turned her attention to Abeke, and when Abeke saw her companion's anxious expression, she realized that her own injuries were the more serious. She pressed her hand against her neck and grimaced when it came back red with blood.

She cautiously turned her head from side to side, and though the movement was painful, it wasn't overly limited. She had a couple of puncture wounds; that was the extent of it. They must have been bleeding so much because they were near her head. She'd had similar injuries before, and she'd gotten over them.

"A rookie mistake," Rollan said ruefully. "We should have realized that more than human hunters would be attracted to this herd of yaks."

"Yes," Abeke said, ripping off a strip from the hem of her shirt and wrapping it tight around her neck. As she did, though, she looked up and saw the mountain lions had regrouped and were going after a new target—the baby yak. It had fallen behind the rest of the herd. Its elderly caretakers stood a few yards away, groaning worriedly but too weak to confront the mountain lions directly.

Normally Abeke would let the natural order take care of itself—maybe this baby yak wasn't meant to live. But then she remembered the jaw around the back of her neck, and Essix's limp wing, and fury rose in her. Her fists clenched and unclenched helplessly. Before she knew it, she'd gotten to her feet. Blinking back light-headedness, she stalked toward the lions, fitting an arrow to her bow.

The panicking little yak was darting this way and that, crying out to its caretakers, begging them to come help him. But the mountain lions were relentless, keeping themselves between the yak and its protectors, edging nearer and nearer to the terrified animal.

Fresh blood was streaming down Abeke's neck, more than she would have expected, and she found it hard to run straight. As she staggered forward, she struggled to string her bow. She wrapped the line around time and again until it held, then pulled an arrow from her quiver with shaking arms. Somewhere behind her, Rollan was calling out, but she couldn't hear him—the whole world was sounding at once, roaring through her head.

The first lion had just made a nip at the baby yak's rear leg when Abeke got near enough to fire. She pulled back the bowstring as quietly as she could, but in her disoriented state, she lost her balance and crushed a stick beneath her heel.

The mountain lions looked up, fully alert, and soon spotted their stalker with her bow and arrow. The little yak looked around in confusion as its would-be killers sped away. Bleating, the baby ran to its elders, and together they headed back to the safety of the herd.

Despite Rollan's cries, Abeke sprinted after the lions. There was a flash of yellow as Uraza cut right in front of her path. What was the leopard trying to do, trip her? "Get out of the way!" Abeke yelled.

But Uraza cut in front of her again, looking up at her with those luminous purple eyes.

More blood ran down her chest, and suddenly the sky was white instead of blue. Abeke staggered forward, sensing Uraza's soft presence at her side as she did. The world began to spin. As she stumbled forward, she became aware of people emerging from the woods all around the clearing, figures with brown skin and thick, braided black hair.

There, too, was the green of the trees, a bed of fallen needles, and that white sky, so white it was cold, a cold that took the world spinning even faster so her feet couldn't stay level upon it, couldn't dig in hard enough to keep her upright.

Abeke fell against warm Uraza, then tumbled onto her back. She tried to force herself upright again, but couldn't.

Her vision turned yellow as Uraza stood directly over her, making a sound Abeke had come to recognize as her protective yowl. Tentatively, Abeke slid out from under the leopard, hand tight on the fabric binding her neck. It was wet with blood.

Abeke couldn't get her eyes to focus. She closed them for a long moment and struggled to open them again. When she did, she had a moment of clear vision and gasped.

She was surrounded by men and women. They were scowling, furs tied around their powerful shoulders. Every last one of them had a spear. And every last one of them had the tip pointed at her.

STONE

STONE WASN'T SILENT. MEILIN REALIZED THAT MUCH AS she trudged along the dark tunnel. There were the sounds she and the others made, of course—Briggan's panting, Kovo's grunts as he knuckle-walked over sharp shards, the syllables of Takoda's meditations, and the soft patter of Conor's boots under the fizzle-splatter of his sparking torch. But the heavy weight all around them made its own noises, too.

Though the stone under their feet wasn't wet, there was water everywhere, running through distant cave systems. Meilin heard constant skittering sounds as small creatures fled, vanishing long before Conor's torchlight reached them.

One time, the escaping creature hadn't sounded small at all. It sounded like footfalls running away—something the size of a human. When they heard it, Meilin cut glances at Conor and Takoda, pointedly avoiding Kovo. Takoda looked back, a finger over his mouth, signaling for silence.

What option did they all have but to continue forward?

The most constant sound was sighing rock. It was a crunching, ominous rumble, like the earth was one huge creature grinding its teeth in a restless sleep. In the darkness, Meilin began to imagine that they were walking down an enormous gullet, that the beast might at any time decide to swallow them all.

So far there hadn't been any options for where to turn, but after sloping downward for a mile, the tunnel branched into two narrow openings. They were in a small, round chamber in the rock, mushrooms along the floor and a puddle of water in the middle. A stalagmite rose from within, covered in moss that gleamed wet and purple in the torchlight.

"Left or right?" Meilin asked.

Takoda shrugged and answered in his soft, melodious voice. "Left and right are not what I'm concerned about. What worries me is that neither Briggan nor Kovo will fit in those tunnels."

Surprising even herself, Meilin whirled on Takoda, rage making her whole body rigid, her hands tightened into fists. "I don't care where Kovo does or does not fit! He's lucky we don't find the narrowest tunnel we can and leave him trapped down here forever."

"Meilin," Conor said in low tones. He placed a tentative hand on her back. "I'm as angry as you are. But we're stuck down here. We'll need one another to get out of this alive. Let's save our fight with Kovo until once we've found the surface."

The fear in Conor's eyes said what his words didn't—there might not *be* a way out.

Kovo met Meilin's gaze challengingly and let out a long, lewd snort, flapping his lips at the end of it so they sprayed spit on her.

"Takoda," Meilin said, her words slow and deliberate, "can you sign to Kovo that if he ever dares do that again, I will smash his brains out with my staff?"

"I don't know those signs," Takoda said with a worried expression.

Meilin missed Rollan all of a sudden. She could really use his sense of humor right now.

"Kovo did save Conor back at the pit," Takoda said. "I'm not trying to defend him, but I don't know why he would do that if his goal all along was to trap us. He made a mistake, that's all."

Seeing the gorilla's glittering, ferociously intelligent eyes, Meilin wasn't so sure Kovo was the type to make mistakes. But as her rage ebbed, she saw Conor's point: They all needed one another if they hoped to survive. The horrible weight of the creaking stone pressing down all around them was putting her on edge. If it's what it took to survive, she'd call a truce with Kovo until she saw the sun again. Whenever that was.

Sighing, Meilin beckoned Conor to the two tunnel entranceways so they could inspect them together. Takoda was right—it would be tricky for the three of them to fit through either one. There was absolutely no way Briggan or Kovo could make it.

"I can bring Briggan into his passive form, of course,"

Conor said. "But . . ." His voice trailed off as he looked at Kovo.

Takoda lowered himself so he sat cross-legged in front of Kovo, staring into the beast's eyes. For a few seconds, Kovo looked everywhere but at Takoda—down both tunnels, up into the ceiling, into the torch reflection in the puddle of dark water. Then finally, sulkily, he met Takoda's eyes.

Meilin was surprised to see not just reluctance in the ape's expression, but something else—a twinge of anxiety.

Takoda made a series of hand gestures, finishing by tracing the spot on Conor's forearm where Briggan went into tattoo form. Takoda traced the same area on his own arm.

Kovo looked up at the ceiling for a long moment. Gradually his gaze shifted back to Takoda, then he bowed his head. His eyes glittered, catching even more of the torchlight. He bared his teeth and suddenly roared, beating his chest with his fists.

Meilin and Conor sprang into action. Conor had his fists clenched, and Meilin held her quarterstaff out in guard position.

"No!" Takoda said, right into Kovo's face.

Meilin wasn't sure if Takoda had been speaking to them or to Kovo. It didn't matter, because it was Kovo who got the message. He lowered his chin to his massive chest and sighed a long, puttering sigh.

Kovo made one sign, tracing laurels on the top of his head. Then he delicately placed his thumb between his teeth and bit it.

"King. Worthless," Takoda translated. He shook his head severely and made the thumb-biting gesture again. "Not worthless."

Kovo looked at the boy for a long moment, misery etched in his face. Then, with a shimmering flash and a popping sound, the ape vanished.

He reappeared, not as a tattoo on Takoda's forearm, but on his chin and neck. The image of a gorilla, charging forward with teeth bared, went from the tip of Takoda's sharp jawline and down his throat, Kovo's foot stepping on the boy's collarbone.

Takoda stared in disbelief where Kovo had just been sitting.

"Congratulations," Meilin said without much enthusiasm. "You and the enemy of Erdas are closer than ever."

"In the spirit of being as honest as I can be with you," Takoda said. "I have to tell you that I *miss* him."

"Then that makes one of us," Conor said. Wincing at his own gibe, Conor cast a guilty glance at Takoda. "But I get what you mean. It's not your fault who you were bonded to. Come on, Briggan."

At the sound of his name, the wolf nuzzled Conor's hand. And then, with another shimmer and pop, Briggan disappeared into tattoo form.

Conor stood before one tunnel and then the other, shining the torch down each in turn. "They look identical to me," he said.

Meilin stood back-to-back with Takoda. "My shoulders are the narrowest of the three of us, just barely. So let me go first and report back. I'll try the left tunnel, because it seems to slope upward. Since we keep hearing those dripping sounds, I'd rather not end up falling into an underground lake."

"Good thinking," Conor said, shuddering. He handed Meilin his torch, then quickly retracted his hand. It was the one with the parasite.

Meilin could only imagine how it would feel to have something like that growing inside of her. Probably not too unlike being bonded to a villain like Kovo, actually. What a state they were all in. She squeezed Conor's shoulder encouragingly. "I'll be fine, don't worry about me."

"Good luck," Takoda said. "We'll be right here if you need help."

At least their conversation had temporarily gotten Meilin's mind off the mass of stone over them. Before her nerves could get the better of her, she started down the tunnel. She had to crouch from the start, but as the path narrowed more, it became clear she'd only be able to move forward on her elbows. She lowered herself onto the smooth rocks of the tunnel floor and began to wriggle her way along.

She smelled something burning and realized it was a piece of her own hair. The fumes from the torch were way too close—she'd have to extinguish it. Reluctantly, she pressed the tip against the tunnel wall until the flame went out.

She continued forward into the tight, constricting darkness.

Weight. That was all Meilin could sense as she wedged one shoulder then the other into the narrow tunnel of rock. Above her were tons of solid, heavy stone. All it would take is one shudder, one tremor in the rock, for it all to collapse on top of her. This giant stone beast would swallow her down.

Focus, Meilin. One arm eased forward, then she wriggled the rest of her body behind. She could feel her body pucker and bruise wherever she passed over even the slightest pebble.

Somewhere behind her, Conor was saying something, but she couldn't hear him—her own body had nearly sealed the tunnel tight. All she wanted was to turn back and see the sky again. But now that the opening had collapsed, they had no other options.

Meilin paused. The rock was grinding again.

Her breath came short, and suddenly her only instinct was to struggle, to push back against the rock, to do whatever she could to fight it off. But if the weight was about to fall in on her, then fighting would only make it happen faster. She martialed all the discipline of her warrior training and forced her body to be still.

She could feel the stone shiver against her, pressing her ribs in tight. Tears welled in Meilin's eyes, and her breath came only in rapid gasps.

Then the pressure relented, and the rock was still. Meilin thought of the stone bridges she had helped build in Zhong, how they would sway—but not fall—as their stones contracted and expanded. Maybe the same thing was happening here. Steadying her breath, she forced herself to continue wriggling forward in the darkness.

The tunnel narrowed even more—how was that possible?

If she continued this way and got wedged tight, how would Conor and Takoda free her? Maybe they wouldn't be able to. She'd starve or die of thirst. If scavenging animals didn't get her first.

Stop it, Meilin. Terror is your enemy.

She continued forward, using the little free space under her hands to brush the tunnel clear as she wriggled, to gain her even the tiny space that the rock dust took up. Her shoulders wedged tight once, and then she managed to free them, her collarbone wrenching painfully before she could continue forward, now with arms down by her sides.

Relief. A cool, sulfurous breeze hit her face. She'd never been so grateful for something so stinky. As Meilin moved forward, her head and shoulders came free into an open space.

Her first impulse was to hurl forward into freedom, but she stopped herself.

She desperately wished she had space to relight the torch. As she eased forward, the top half of her body was hanging in the sulfurous open air, but her hands were still pressed into her sides. She flailed around, hoping to contact a nearby ledge or bit of ground. But it was all open. What would she do now? She might be a couple of feet above the ground, or the bottom could be hundreds of feet away.

Meilin figured it was best to lean down as far as she could manage and use her fingertips to test whether there was any ground beneath. Leaving the torch pinned against her waist, she wrenched her hands free and felt down and all around. There was nothing below. She'd have to use her feet instead, which would reach farther.

Once enough of her was free, she reversed her grip and eased her legs out. Now her feet dangled low, while only the strength of her fingertips prevented her from falling. She felt a sudden need to summon Jhi, to have the comfort of her companion. But Jhi couldn't fit into the tunnel, and the idea of summoning the panda into open air and watching her plummet was too horrifying to consider.

"Conor?" Meilin called.

She heard his faint reply from the far end of the tunnel. "Yes?"

She realized there was nothing she could ask him for. What would happen next was all up to fate. "Wish me luck!" she called.

"What's happening?" came his distant voice.

"Just wish me luck!"

Meilin stretched her toes, hoping to contact ground. No success. Her fingers began to strain. Then, unexpectedly, a rock came free under one hand and slipped away.

She free-fell for a long second, then struck something soft. Meilin heard a ghastly cry from beneath her and rolled off whatever living thing she'd hit. Something was panting near her.

Then she felt a hand on her chin.

Shouting in panic, Meilin reeled backward, flailing in the darkness. She fell from whatever perch she'd been on. She dropped for another horrible moment, then struck pebbly ground and something wet.

Meilin staggered desperately through the darkness, hands outstretched. She contacted another warm body, smooth and hairless and strangely oily, and kicked out. The creature, whatever it was, gasped and fell back. Meilin turned in a slow circle, looking all around her but finding only blackness, fists out and ready to strike. "Hello?" she said.

"What do you see?" Conor called.

The torch! Of course—there was a second torch at her waist! Cursing herself, she patted her waist until she found the handle, then struggled to free it.

Before she could light it, though, more hands were on her. They clutched and pulled, tearing her skin. Then sharp fingernails were on her face, yanking at her ears, scraping her cheeks.

Meilin screamed.

THE MANY

CONOR PACED HELPLESSLY, THEN HELD STILL WHEN HE heard Meilin screaming from the far side of the tunnel. When he called out for her and she didn't respond, he prepared to leap into the shaft. "Takoda!" he cried. "Follow me!"

"If Meilin is in trouble," Takoda said behind him, "whatever happened to her will happen to you, too. Think, Conor!"

"I don't care about being reasonable! She needs us!" Conor yelled, whirling with his second torch.

The ruddy light illuminated Takoda's face dramatically, casting shadows down the gorilla tattoo stretching along his neck. "If she's been attacked, you'll head into it face-first, with no way to defend yourself," Takoda said.

"You have more in common with Kovo than you think," Conor snapped. "We're going now!"

Takoda nodded wearily. "I was afraid you wouldn't budge. Okay, let's head in."

Conor handed the torch to Takoda and had begun to wriggle through the tunnel again when Takoda grabbed his ankle.

"Hold on," Takoda said. "Do you hear something?"

Conor realized he could hear scuffling sounds farther along in the tunnel. "Meilin?" he called out. "Is that you?"

The scuffling got nearer.

"Meilin?" Conor called again.

Still no answer. "Back up, back up!" Conor screamed at Takoda.

As Takoda scrambled out of the tunnel behind him, Conor did his best to wriggle in reverse, hustling as fast as he could.

They came free into the chamber, where Takoda pulled in front of Conor and brandished the torch.

A figure, just Meilin's height and weight, raced toward them. "Oh, thank Tellun, Meilin, you're—"

But it wasn't Meilin.

Conor and Takoda fell backward in terror as a scrawny human figure scrabbled out of the tunnel on all fours, its twisted yellow fingernails clicking against the stone ground. It was a ghastly gray-white, with barely a hair on its head. Its eyes were wide and pink, and before Conor's eyes the giant black pupils contracted to pinpoints—the torchlight seemed to have the monster dazzled. It froze, its long, skinny arms dragging on the ground.

"What is that?" Conor whispered, reeling backward.

"I don't know," Takoda whispered back, fear tightening his voice. "But look at its forehead."

Conor had assumed it was dirt, but could see clearly now that the creature had a symbol on its forehead—a spiral, just like the one on Zerif's forehead, and on his own arm. He had no time to reflect on it, though, as at that moment another of the strange creatures emerged from the tunnel—then a third, and a fourth.

"We have to get out of here!" Takoda yelled.

"What about Meilin?" Conor said.

This time, the creatures heard them. They pressed their milky eyelids shut and lunged at the boys blindly, clawlike fingernails outstretched, clashing whenever they struck the chamber's stone walls. Conor and Takoda instinctively fell back, tumbling to the ground and scuttling backward on all fours.

Whether summoned by Takoda or appearing from his own will, Kovo was suddenly back among them. With a pop, the gorilla appeared in the round chamber, seizing the torch where Takoda had dropped it in one clean motion. He stood over the kids protectively, the flaming light tight in his strong black hand. Now that their eyes were closed, however, the creatures were no longer scared of the light. They lurched toward them, slowly circling the round cavern, easing closer and closer. Mightily as Kovo swung the torch, it did nothing to keep them at bay.

All the while, more and more monsters emerged from the tunnel.

One of them contacted Conor, wrapping a clammy and surprisingly strong hand around his wrist. Conor cried out and whirled in an attempt to break free. The creature gnashed its sharp teeth in the air, trying to get them around his forearm.

Takoda had a slender knife out—his only weapon—and stepped toward the monsters, slashing wildly. Kovo roared and motioned for them to return to his side. Though in any other situation he'd have been reluctant to take orders from his former enemy, Conor willingly pressed his back tight against Kovo's, while Takoda did the same.

Kovo wrapped one strong hand around the leg of the nearest ghoulish creature and, with a grunt, whipped it into the air, flailing the limp form into the surrounding monsters. Then Kovo threw the lifeless body to one side, roaring and beating on his chest.

The torch tumbled away in the process, and Conor scrambled to pick it up. As he did, one of the monsters leaped onto his back. Conor staggered about, backing into walls, desperately trying to free himself. But more creatures continued to pour out of the tunnel. Another latched on to Conor's back while he was still fighting off the first.

With a furious roar, Kovo set himself on the creatures thronging them, one powerful arm plucking monsters from Conor and the other from Takoda. As Kovo bent over in his task, three of the ghouls leaped onto the gorilla's back, with more behind them clamoring to get on. Even mighty Kovo staggered under their combined weight, bleeding from multiple bites.

Conor summoned Briggan. The wolf appeared in midair and leaped to the attack, whirling and lunging as best he could in the close quarters of the dark cave, dancing in and out of the torchlight as he pounced and wheeled, pale ghastly creatures falling under his jaws time and again.

Kovo used the surprise of Briggan's appearance to press the offensive, reaching to the ground and heaving up whatever debris his hands found on the cave floor. Heaps of rock flew into the air, strafing their attackers. But more and more creatures continued to pour through the tunnel.

"Meilin!" Conor yelled. She'd been right where these monsters emerged from, and the thought of it filled his heart with icy dread. Conor couldn't stand to imagine what the ghouls had already done to her. "Too many to fight!" he gasped. "We need to retreat before they block the tunnel to the surface."

"They'll easily chase us down!" said Takoda.

One of the creatures got its jaw around Kovo's ankle. The gorilla roared in pain, nearly losing his footing before Briggan managed to hurl it away. But Briggan was having trouble of his own: A creature ripped its sharp yellow fingernails into his ear. The wolf's blood gleamed in the torchlight.

Conor felt his own flesh tear as one of the beasts clawed at his throat. It was all he could do to jam its forehead away with the heel of a hand, but as he did his fingers slid into the creature's open mouth. If it clamped its sharp teeth down, Conor might lose them all in one bite.

The creature began to bite down.

But then the world filled with light.

Dazzled, Conor looked up into the blinding white flash, blinking as he whisked his hand free. Tears streamed down his face. He couldn't see anything beyond the afterglow that had burned purple into his vision. He heard Briggan whining in pain nearby and staggered toward the sound, finally making contact with his spirit animal's coarse fur. Kovo panted nearby, and Conor could hear Takoda groaning not far away.

Conor's eyes gradually adjusted enough that the cave resolved into view. Lavender light seeped from a stone lying in the middle of a puddle on the cavern's floor. Conor realized it was some strange kind of flare, giving off ever-weakening light.

The light bomb seemed to affect the ghoulish creatures much more strongly. They were laid out flat on the floor, whimpering and quivering, fingers clamped over their eyes. Already the first was struggling to regain its feet in the dwindling light.

"Up here!" came a female voice high above them, on the far side of the cavern.

Conor looked up, shielding his eyes as best he could from the painful lavender glow. A slender figure stood at the edge of a hole high up in the cavern's ceiling. "Meilin? Is that you?" Conor asked, confused.

"No," the girl said. "No time to explain—these monsters won't be stunned for much longer. Hurry up!"

Still dazed, Conor watched the girl lower a rope down the twenty feet or so from the entrance. With a familiar pop, Briggan disappeared into his tattoo. "Takoda!" Conor said. "Get Kovo into his passive state! Hurry!"

Takoda bit his lip. "I'm trying!"

Kovo took it into his hands—literally. He placed his large, hairy fists on top of Takoda's shoulders and stared deeply into the boy's eyes. Then Takoda gasped, like he'd been punched, and in a flash Kovo became a tattoo on the boy's neck. Conor shook his head. *Of course* it would be Kovo who got to decide precisely where to become a tattoo—and then place himself in such a prominent position.

The two boys stepped over the moaning and shifting bodies, stealing toward the rope. Conor gave it one tug to test it, and then held it out to Takoda. The slender boy easily clambered up. Conor followed, working his way up the slick length of braided fiber, all the way to the top. He hurled himself over the edge and sprawled out flat, gasping for breath.

"No rest yet," the mysterious girl said, still only a silhouette before Conor's seared retinas. "Help me pull this up, quick!"

Conor couldn't find the strength to stand but he rolled onto his belly and, together with Takoda and the girl, heaved on the rope. A creature had just reached it as they whisked it up. The ghastly beast beat its fists against the cavern wall in frustration.

Conor lay on his back, gasping. He couldn't muster the strength to resist when the girl removed one of the torches from his belt and lit it.

"What a marvelous thing, these lights," she said. Clearly the illumination was painful for her. Although she closed her eyes to slits, they streamed tears, even in the dim light.

When Conor propped himself up, he saw a girl about his own age and pale as ether, with short white hair and eyes that were a soft pink. She was like a beautiful, delicate version of the creatures below. Even so, Conor found himself staggering back against the tunnel wall in fear, preparing to summon Briggan.

"It's okay," came a voice Conor knew as well as his own. "She's a friend."

Conor gave a sob of relief.

Meilin crept into the torchlight, a smile on her face. "I fell right into the nest of those things. Xanthe swept down from above and helped me out on one of her rope ladders. These caverns are honeycombed with passages above. She knows all of them. We had to go the long way around, and raced through the tunnels to the top of the cavern as soon as we could."

"You were attacked by the beings my people call the Many," the girl said in a delicate and unfamiliar accent. "The only defenses we have against them are our tunnels. There's a whole system of ladders and traps. You wouldn't have stood a chance, two boys against all of them."

She doesn't know we have spirit animals, Conor realized. On instinct, he decided to keep Briggan and Kovo a secret until he knew more about this mysterious girl. Takoda clearly had the same thought: He slyly buttoned his borrowed green cloak tight, so that its cowl hid his neck up to the chin.

"What *are* those things?" Conor asked.

"You saw the symbol on their foreheads? They used to be like my people, but they . . . changed. There will be time later to explain, but it's not safe to linger in the territory of the Many. Please, come with me."

Conor's stomach dropped, though he tried to hide it. Seeing those monsters might have been seeing his own future. Trying to keep his terror out of his face, he shot a look at Meilin and Takoda. *Not any other option but going along with her, is there?* They shot him similar glances back.

Before they headed up the tunnel, Meilin clasped Conor close to her. "I'm so glad you're okay," she said loudly. Then she whispered: "Keep the spirit animals a secret."

She'd had the same instinct as he and Takoda.

They passed down the tunnel, Xanthe taking the lead, crouching and moving ably forward on all fours. She wore a simple charcoal-colored shift, woven from some shimmering material that Conor had never seen before. She carried no weapons that he could see.

He took in her white-pale skin. Even though this stranger had saved their lives, Conor found it hard to blot the monsters Xanthe had called the Many from his mind.

As they crept down the tunnels, Xanthe looked back admiringly at the torch in Conor's hand, though it still made her eyes stream tears. "Such a marvelous thing. All the lights we have down here are so temporary in comparison."

Conor smiled and shook his head. "I never thought a torch was that special. We have so many of them where we're from."

"Where is that?" Xanthe asked, her tone studied and neutral.

"Aboveground," Meilin said.

Xanthe stopped, hands clasped in front of her mouth. Her eyes shone with awe. "That's what I'd hoped. But I hadn't dared assume it."

"Why is being from above so special?" Conor asked.

"Because it's been a thousand years since anyone traveled here from the surface," Xanthe said. "You've come to stop the Wyrm, as my people have long hoped. We've been waiting centuries for you to save us. Welcome to the land of Sadre."

10

THE HEALER

TRY AS SHE MIGHT, ABEKE COULDN'T MAKE THE WORDS she was hearing come together into anything that had meaning. In front of her wavering vision, so close to her nose that it appeared double, a spear tip trembled in the air. Abeke held perfectly still—partly to keep the armed tribespeople calm, and partly because of the puncture wound on her neck. Uraza was hunched protectively over her torso, making low warning growls and batting away any spear tips that came too near.

Keeping her hands open along the ground to prove she wasn't reaching for a weapon, Abeke lowered her head and placed her hopes in Rollan.

Essix wheeled above, giving an occasional falcon cry, so Abeke knew that Rollan must be near. He was probably hiding at the forest line, waiting to see if it was safe before he came forward.

"Hello, there!" she heard Rollan call.

Or not.

Instantly, half the spear tips disappeared from Abeke's vision, warriors grunting as they prepared to hurl their weapons.

If this standoff came to battle, Abeke needed to be ready. Gritting her teeth, hoping she wouldn't pass out, Abeke grabbed the nearest spear shaft and yanked. The weapon didn't come free, but she was able to pull herself up it so she was on her feet. Instantly, though, the world buckled under her, and she was back down on her knees. Uraza stood over her, growling to warn off any attackers.

"Hold!" Rollan called. "We mean you no trouble!"

The tribespeople conferred with one another in their own language, then one of them spoke in Common. "Drop your weapon, stranger."

"I'll drop mine if you drop yours," Rollan called.

"Do as they say, Rollan," Abeke managed to croak. "I'm in no condition to fight, and we need their help."

She heard a thud as Rollan sighed and dropped his dagger. From high above, Essix shrieked indignantly. Giving in easily wasn't her or Rollan's style.

"Thank you," said the same voice. A woman knelt into Abeke's vision. She had a sun-wrinkled face, a striking mixture of tans and ruddy reds, and surprisingly kind eyes. An infant was wrapped tightly to her chest with a length of yak hide, only the top of its head poking out.

Uraza struck out at the woman with her paw. Her claws were retracted, but it served as a warning from getting too near. Though the woman didn't appear scared, she crept backward so she was a safe distance away.

"My name is Aynar," she said. "My son is the healer for our people. But he's back at camp, so I'm the best we have for now. Your wound will not heal on its own. Rot can easily set into mountain lion bites. If you allow me, I would tend the wound on your neck, Abeke of Okaihee."

Abeke startled. "You know my name!"

"I wasn't sure until you said Rollan's name," the woman said, giving Abeke an apologetic smile. "I hope you will forgive the spears pointed in your direction. Word has reached us that Erdas has again entered a troubled time. Greetings, too, Rollan of Concorba. You are both legends here. We suspected who you were immediately—it's not every day, after all, that one comes across a leopard prowling here."

"No autographs, please," Rollan said wryly.

"You should move as little as possible," Aynar continued to Abeke. "Our horses are on the other side of this grove. With your blessing, we'll fetch them and rig a litter to carry you to our camp. It's only a few miles off."

Rollan knelt beside the woman, taking in Abeke's injury and giving her a worried smile. His expression was enough to tell Abeke he was willing to go along with Aynar's plan.

"Thank you for helping us," Abeke said.

Aynar nodded and started giving orders in the tribal language. Once the hunters were out of view, Rollan plopped down beside Abeke. "Huh. Not two days into our Amayan journey and we already need rescuing."

"Sorry," Abeke said, gingerly prodding the wound on her neck. "It's not like I *meant* for that mountain lion to maul me."

At the mention of Abeke's attacker, Uraza gave an angry growl. Abeke affectionately tousled the fluff of hair sticking up on the back of Uraza's neck, and the leopard relaxed.

"What we need most is information," Rollan said. "Maybe this tribe knows about the summoned Great Beast. When you think about it, your injury might have been a brilliant move."

"Hard to see it that way at the moment," Abeke said, wincing.

The tribespeople returned with a litter rigged behind one of their horses. They'd taken a birch canoe, tied one end to the saddle, and attached two wooden discs to the low end so that it could roll. "Come," Aynar said to Abeke. "Lie inside."

The world bloomed white as Rollan helped Abeke to her feet, but her friend's arm under her shoulders was strong and firm as he got her to the litter and gently arranged her inside. Aynar removed the blood-soaked fabric binding Abeke's neck and used a flat, smooth stick to apply a poultice that stung at first but soon suffused Abeke with a cool, fresh feeling. Aynar lightly draped a soft rabbit's hide over the wound.

Now that her pain had lessened, all Abeke wanted was to fall asleep. With the last of her energy, she called Uraza into passive state for the journey. Though the leopard was swift, she wouldn't be able to keep up with horses over a long distance. Abeke sleepily watched Rollan mount Aynar's steed behind her, and then passed out. Even though the litter bumped and dragged, she didn't wake up until they came to a stop.

That poultice must have had something powerful in it; when she opened her eyes, Abeke felt like herself again. She untied the rawhide strands attaching her to the litter and rolled over the side, easily getting to her feet. She could hear no one around: They must have decided to let her sleep late into the day.

The tribe's camp was a scattering of large tents, each crafted from slender logs with animal hide stretched over. The grass around each tent was fresh and untrampled, which made Abeke think they hadn't been set up for long. Maybe the tribe moved every day, or every couple of days. The nomad tribes in the north of Nilo were much the same. They avoided a lot of the problems that plagued those who lived in villages—lice, parasites, scavengers—by bedding somewhere new every night.

The sky was so large up here. When Abeke squinted her eyes, it was almost like she was below the same wide blue sky that stretched above Okaihee. Just seeing its expansiveness invigorated her. She hoped that after she and Rollan had tracked down this Great Beast, Lenori would augur the next one in Nilo. Abeke longed to see her father and sister again.

"I see you're feeling better," came a quiet voice. Abeke turned to see a boy of about eleven emerge from the smallest tent. His skin was dark, nearly as dark as Abeke's, though his cheeks were a pink red, almost the color of salmon. His hair was tied back in a single braid that went down his back, and his eyes were a startling color—light orange-brown, like the rind of a cheese.

"You're Aynar's son, the tribe's healer," Abeke said. Something about the gentleness in the boy's eyes had made it clear.

"I am," he said, with an uneasy tilt to his head.

"Forgive me," Abeke said, "but aren't you a little young for that responsibility?"

"You were not that much older than me when you went to fight with the Greencloaks," the boy said, smiling. "But you are correct. I was named healer only recently. There were special circumstances. In any case, our word for 'healer' has a much broader set of meanings than it does in the Common language."

"It does?"

At Abeke's interest, the boy's previous shyness melted away. "Our healers are also moral guides. We conduct listening ceremonies to help our people find their hearts. The other boys hunt, but that doesn't interest me much at all."

Abeke experimented with her neck, angling her head from side to side. Miraculously, she was able to do so without pain. The clean scent of pine rose from her fresh bandages. "I'm glad it doesn't," Abeke said. "You have real talent—what's your name?"

The boy beamed with pride. "Anda. My mother gave you a poultice I made. I always send the hunters out with it, and it appears to have done its work. While you were sleeping, I added another. This new one should speed the healing even more, and prevent scarring."

"Where is Rollan?" Abeke asked.

"Hunting with the men. They would have loved for you to join them—it's a rare opportunity to learn from such a famous hunter—but you were asleep. So Rollan went instead. He . . . did not seem comfortable riding. I've never seen a horse take such an instant disliking to someone."

"He has that effect on horses," Abeke said with a smile. "And walruses. And some people. Is there anything to eat?"

"Of course," Anda said, blushing. "I should have offered earlier."

Abeke chewed strips of salty yak jerky while Anda walked her around the camp. It was small—only five large tents circling a fire. Two horses, so scrawny they were probably used for carrying supplies and not riders, grazed nearby.

After warning Anda, Abeke summoned Uraza. The leopard nuzzled Abeke affectionately, then sniffed worriedly at her wounded neck. She was clearly relieved by what she found. Uraza bounded and pranced, undoubtedly hunting for more butterflies—until she noticed Anda.

Uraza stood stock-still, staring at the boy with her large lavender eyes. Then she did something Abeke had never seen Uraza do before: The leopard lay down in the earth, head resting on her paws, and stared up at him.

"She likes you," Abeke said. But her voice trailed off, because she could see that it was more than that. The expression in Uraza's eyes was closer to submission.

"Should we show her?" Anda asked the open air. Abeke whirled around, but couldn't see what or who Anda was talking to.

Uraza purred loudly, at full attention as she stared into the nearby tree line.

Abeke followed the leopard's gaze and saw, camouflaged in a copse of pine trees, an elk.

A very large elk. It stood motionless, noble head held high, antlers as broad as a man's arms. Its fur was tinged with white and gold, the same mix of colors as Anda's striking eyes.

The elk's eyes locked on Anda, then it stepped out toward them, its gait stately and unhurried.

"You summoned Tellun," Abeke said in awe.

"You make him sound so serious." Anda laughed. "I just think of him as my elk. And I'm his boy."

As the noble elk drew near, there was no shred of doubt in Abeke's mind that she was in the presence of Tellun, the leader of all the Great Beasts. Uraza looked at him with wide, awestruck eyes, confirming Abeke's thoughts.

Without quite knowing why, Abeke got to her knees.

"Please get up! There's no need to do that!" Anda said. "My elk is silly most of the time; I'm not sure why he's being so serious today . . ." Anda's voice trailed off, and his lips moved silently instead. It looked like he was communicating with the elk. Anda's light brown eyes widened, and his jaw set tight.

"Why didn't you ever tell me you were *that* important?" he asked.

When the hunters returned, Abeke, Anda, Uraza, and Tellun himself were quietly waiting at the edge of the camp. They watched the dust cloud gradually settle as the hunters brought their horses to a halt.

"Abeke!" Rollan said as he struggled to dismount from his horse, then struggled even harder to extract his foot from the stirrup. "I wish you had been with us. Apparently I've already lost all my saddle callouses—ouch—but I used a *bow*! And I wasn't half bad. I mean I wasn't Abeke-level or anything, but . . ."

Rollan's eyes widened, and he went pale. Just like Abeke, he, too, dropped to his knees when he realized he was in the presence of Tellun.

The noble elk maintained his serene gaze, but Abeke suspected she saw a wink in his eyes.

Aynar dismounted and approached, arm in arm with a tall, severe-looking man. He had his hair in a long braid, like Anda's, but his was striped with gray. If his face had ever had any of Anda's gentleness, it had lost it long ago. Abeke sensed she was seeing the boy's father.

"I see our guests have met Tellun," Aynar said. Beside her, Anda's father watched the elk warily.

"The Great Beasts have returned to Erdas," Abeke said. "Your son has had a tremendous honor come to him."

"The type of honor that also destroys all of our tribe's privacy," Anda's father muttered.

Abeke frowned. She remembered her own bonding ceremony, when she'd summoned Uraza—the leopard had brought a deluge of life-giving rain to her parched village. At the time, Abeke had thought she'd become her village's new Rain Dancer. Her father had responded to that news with surprising skepticism. Though she and her family had worked through their differences, Abeke watched a similar defensiveness settle into Anda's father's features.

Because of what she'd been through with her own family, though, she understood it: He wanted to believe all of this was impossible, so the tribe's life could remain the way it had always been.

While the other hunters dismounted, silent with reverence, Aynar inspected Abeke's wound. "I never would have thought that you'd be standing, much less walking around, by the time we came back. Anda, your skills have improved so much, my son."

Abeke ran a hand over the bandage on the back of her neck. "I can barely feel any pain. It's amazing. I hope Anda gets to meet Jhi someday. They could learn a lot from each other."

"They could gossip in the women's tent and sip herbal teas together," Anda's father said.

Rollan cut him a severe look. "A talented healer can turn the tide of a military campaign far more effectively than even the strongest warrior. I've seen it happen."

Anda's father shook his head curtly and tightened the strap of his quiver with a savage jerk. "Do not pretend to educate me on battle. You should know your place—maybe children rule in Greenhaven, but not here."

"There are more important concerns for us to talk about," Abeke said, stepping between the two. "A man named Zerif is on the loose, hunting down the Great Beasts as they return to the world." She cast a worried look at Anda. "Severing them from their human partners."

"I knew we should not trust these outsiders," said Anda's gruff father. "Don't you see, Aynar—they have come to take our son away."

Aynar looked deep into Anda's eyes. "Is that true? You will have to leave?"

Anda couldn't meet his mother's gaze. "It won't be safe for any of us if I stay here. Abeke tells me that Zerif is very powerful, and getting stronger with every Great Beast he claims."

"I'm sorry, Aynar," Abeke said. "I know that your tribe named Anda as its healer precisely because of the good omen when he summoned Tellun. I, too, left my family after I summoned Uraza. I know how painful this is, but believe me when I tell you that I'm closer to my family now than I ever was before I left Okaihee. I've learned so much about myself, and them, while I was away. Anda will return to you even more talented—and even wiser."

"Zerif is undoubtedly on his way," Rollan said. "Even with the help of Uraza and Essix and all your hunters, we'd be stupid to fight him. Your son's best hope—and the best hope for Erdas—is for him to come with us to Greenhaven."

Aynar's eyes filled with tears as she looked at her son. "You've made up your mind. I can see it."

Anda grimaced. "The whole tribe is in danger while Tellun and I stay."

Aynar let out a long sigh and took a step backward. She gathered herself, love and anguish beaming from her eyes as she fought to hold herself together. "I only ask two things of you, my precious son: Do everything you can to keep yourself safe, and return to us once you are able. I'll think of you every time the first star comes out at night."

"And I'll think of you, Mother," Anda said, tears streaming down his face.

At the sight of his son's crying, Anda's father's face tightened into a frown. But he stepped to Anda and clasped him to his chest. "Please don't forget our people's ways when you're on the outside. You will always have a place in our tribe."

"I won't, Father," Anda said. "I'll make you and the rest of the village proud."

"Keep working on your spear arm," his father said.

Anda nodded, struggling to meet his father's eyes.

"Come, let's go," Abeke said sorrowfully. "We have no way of knowing when Zerif will close in."

As Anda shuffled over to join them, Rollan threw his arm around Anda's shoulders. "Wait until you see the healing poultices the Greencloaks have come up with," he whispered. "You're going to be amazed. You can spend your time in Greenhaven practicing whatever you want."

With one bound, Tellun was at Anda's side. Abeke watched in astonishment as the leader of the Great Beasts gave Anda an affectionate lick along the side of his face. He then pressed his side against Anda's, as if to shoulder some of the boy's weight.

PHOS ASTOS

CONOR AND HIS COMPANIONS MOVED SWIFTLY THROUGH winding stone tunnels. The type of rock varied as they traveled—sometimes they were surrounded by speckled granite, sometimes soft, pockmarked limestone, sometimes slippery obsidian. Their footfalls—and the footfalls of other unknown creatures creeping in the dark—reverberated through the tight spaces.

Without the noise of the world above to fill the air, the quiet music of the earth sighed in Conor's ears. The creaking of rock was constant, but there were also rivulets of water trickling somewhere deep inside the stone, beneath the muttering breezes of damp, cool air.

Conor kept his torch lit, but somehow Xanthe was able to see clearly even when she scouted ahead of its light. She'd call out directions to them from much farther along. By the time the companions managed to reach her, Conor would be amazed to see that Xanthe had already clambered up slick passageways and scaled cave walls in the darkness.

Whenever Xanthe pulled far ahead, she sang an ethereal, tuneless song so the others could locate her. The song grew louder and louder until eventually Conor would turn a corner and find the pale girl waiting, perched on a rock or a giant toadstool, her head cocked at a quizzical angle. Then she'd wordlessly continue on her way.

Seen from behind, Xanthe looked even more like the strange beings that had attacked them—the ones she'd called the Many. In Conor's spooked imaginings, her short white hair resembled their bald heads, and her narrow frame was ghastly instead of elegant. But then whenever she'd turn to face them, he'd see the goodwill in her eyes as she beckoned them forward.

"You're all doing very well," Xanthe said cheerfully as she led them splashing through an underground stream. "Before the trouble with the Wyrm, we sent occasional patrols upside to scout. They always came back telling stories of how oafish the upsiders were. You three—well, you're not at the level of Sadreans, but you're still good climbers."

"Thank you?" Meilin said dryly as she heaved herself over a boulder, landing in a few inches of slimy water.

To Conor's surprise, Meilin allowed Xanthe to help her to her feet. "We're almost halfway there now," Xanthe said. "We'll be at Phos Astos before too long."

"What's Phos Astos?" Takoda asked.

"That is a joke, right?" Xanthe called over her shoulder.

"Um, no," Takoda said.

Xanthe stopped short in the tunnel, and the other three nearly piled into her. "Are you telling me you know that little about this land? We have guarded Erdas for centuries."

It did sound pretty bad when she put it that way.

Conor looked to Meilin. If any of them would have been taught about this place, it was her. But even she reluctantly nodded her head.

Xanthe shook her head when she saw their bewildered reactions. "There used to be many of us, but the last few months . . ." She trailed off. "Let me start closer to the beginning. Phos Astos is one of many underground cities settled by my people. These tunnels pass under Erdas, all the way to its farthest corners. Our cities are connected by paths carved out over millennia by ancient rivers and the roots of the Evertree, and we once traded resources along those routes. Until recently." She let out a long sigh. "The Many are *our people*, twisted by an infection that turns into something more like . . . occupation once it reaches their foreheads."

Unable to stifle a gasp, Conor put a hand to his sleeve. The gray creature had been just past his elbow the last time he'd checked. Once it finished its climb, would he end up like one of those monsters?

"We've lost all contact with the other cities of Sadre," Xanthe said. She swallowed, and when she spoke again her voice shook. "Our fear is that they've all succumbed to the infection. Phos Astos might be the last remnant of our civilization."

Meilin fell back a step so that, out of Xanthe's view, she could squeeze Conor's hand. Her message was double: *It's going to be okay* and *Don't say anything*.

"Oh!" Xanthe said as she sighted something in the

distance. "We're nearly there. Now's when we stop going forward and start going down."

"Down?" Conor asked, stomach tightening.

"Down?" Takoda repeated.

"Yes, down," Xanthe said, breaking into a sudden sprint. "Like this!"

She glided forward into the darkness, her white skin and hair shining long after her black shift had merged into the surrounding gloom. Then, in an instant, she dropped away. She simply disappeared.

"Um, can anyone tell me what just happened?" Takoda asked.

"I don't know," Meilin said, creeping forward. "Xanthe? Are you there?"

Torch brandished, Conor took the lead as they eased toward the spot where Xanthe had disappeared. "Oh, wow," he breathed.

Warm air rushed upward in front of him, like in a chimney. They were at the brink of a chasm, glossy black stone extending down as far as the torchlight went. Conor closed his eyes and smiled; the rising air smelled vaguely like the hot stones his mother had once used to warm his bed when he'd come back from shepherding during the brutal Euran winters.

"She just jumped?" Takoda asked. "Into this stream of air?"

"Maybe . . ." Meilin said, finger tapping her lips as she puzzled it out. "My tutors taught me about air currents. If the upward draft can compensate for a body's downward acceleration due to grav—"

Meilin broke off, dumbfounded, as Takoda pivoted so his back was to the chasm, cheerfully waved good-bye, and let himself fall backward. He was there, and then he was gone, as simple as that.

Conor and Meilin stared at each other, beyond words.

Takoda's voice rose up through the hum of the updraft. "Guys, this is *amazing*!"

"We've all gone crazy," Meilin said. "Maybe there's some gas in the air that's making us all—"

Conor stepped off the edge. "Bye, Meilin!" he called up against the hot wind.

At first he fell rapidly, but the moment he let his arms out wide, the updraft caught him and it was like he was barely falling at all. His torch winked out, leaving him in darkness as he gently descended.

"I can't believe you just did that. I'll kill you once I catch up!" Meilin shouted down.

Conor smiled as he imagined her outraged expression. As he continued to descend, he made out Takoda's voice: "Conor, is that you? You're about to hit a net. Xanthe and I will get you out."

Conor rolled over so he was looking down. The dark air wavered in the heat, but very far below, like at the waking edge of a dream, he saw a muted glow. The horizon was a soft, gauzy pink.

Clearly Conor's floating was about to end, but he wished it wouldn't. He hadn't realized how oppressive the squat tunnels of Sadre had been until they'd opened up. There was so much space around him now, and so much clean air—he never wanted to go back to that claustrophobia.

"Okay, see him?" Xanthe said somewhere in the darkness.

Black lines began to trace themselves over the glow from below. They grew bigger and bigger until Conor was caught in some sort of net, a lattice of the same woven material as Xanthe's shift. As soon as he hit it, slender hands reached from the side to grasp him, and then before he knew it Xanthe and Takoda had pulled him off.

They were seated on the far edge of the net. The open spaces between the mushroomy rope led to the ground far below, but the net was sturdy enough that he didn't feel afraid.

"Isn't this amazing, Conor?" Takoda asked. "To think we're the only people from the surface to have ever seen this place!"

In his excitement, Takoda lost his balance. The rope netting pouched beneath his feet, sending him sliding into Xanthe. Both muttered flustered apologies, and Conor noted with amusement how extra vivid Xanthe's blush was against her pale skin.

As the two carefully extracted themselves, Conor looked down through the netting. Now that the updraft wasn't marbling the air, he could see more of the vista below.

They were suspended at the top of a glittering cavern, the ground at least a hundred feet below. The soft pink glow was from mushrooms—many, many mushrooms. The tallest soared as high as Euran oldwood trees and were ringed by shorter mushrooms, which were ringed by even shorter, until the ground at the edge was dusted with a fringe of fungus. All of them gave off the same dull pink light that illuminated the people walking below. The sheer majesty of the cavern was enough to take Conor's breath away.

"Xanthe," he breathed. "This is Phos Astos?"

Xanthe gave him a sly smile by way of an answer, then sat up on the net, expertly swinging her body so that she bounced along with her hands gripping the edge. Heedless of the hundred-foot drop, she leaned far over the side. Seeing her close to tumbling into the wide open space, Conor reeled with vertigo. There was so little separating him from the air below—just these slim black filaments.

"It's perfectly safe," Xanthe said, watching his expression. "There's another net below this one. Just watch me, and then do what I do. Ready? One—" She was interrupted by a familiar voice.

"Conor?" called Meilin. Conor turned in time to see her float down the stream of hot air. She face-planted into the net, then turned to glare at them furiously.

"Hey, Meilin," Conor called. "Hold on, we'll come bring you over."

"Stay where you are," she called warningly. "I'll come to you." Meilin looked down and shrieked when she saw the open space beneath her. She began to creep along the netting, nervously testing her weight on each section of the net before proceeding. Once she'd reached her friends, she closed her eyes and held her knees tight to her chest, keeping herself as compact as possible. "How do we get down?" she asked in a small voice.

"Are you scared of heights, Meilin?" Conor asked. At first his tone was mischievous, but became serious as he realized how scared she was.

"I just want to be on the ground," she said, not opening her eyes.

"We'll be on solid ground in a moment," Xanthe said, smiling encouragingly. "Let me warn my people that you'll be arriving."

Putting her delicate fingers to her mouth, Xanthe let out a high-pitched whistle.

To Conor's surprise, more people began to emerge from the mushrooms themselves, revealing wide openings in the trunks that towered over the cave floor like great trees.

Their skin was the same luminous white as Xanthe's, and they all had short hair of the palest blond. They held still at the entrances, staring up at Conor and the others with startled pink eyes. There were hundreds of them already, and more were emerging every second. Men and women, children and elderly, tall and short—all looked up in wonder.

"Don't be afraid!" Xanthe called down. "These people have come from the surface! They're friends!"

Shocked whispers went through the crowd, then more and more of the Sadreans emerged from their mushroom homes. "Tayne," Xanthe yelled to the nearest, a small, pale boy peering out an opening at the top of the tallest mushroom, "go tell the elders! We're coming down."

The boy waved at Xanthe, then nodded and called something in an unknown language. He then clambered ably down rungs that had been carved into the mushroom flesh. Wherever he placed his hands, he blocked some of the mushroom's pink glow, sending flickering patterns of light onto the cavern's obsidian walls.

Xanthe smiled at the companions' awestruck expressions, obviously pleased by the effect Phos Astos was having on them. "Take it all in," she said. "You won't get a better of view of it than from way up above."

Pink was the city's dominant color, but as Conor's eyes adjusted he saw that there were greens and yellows, too. The mushrooms had some other colorful fungus growing upon them, so that great swaths of glittering color spread all the way up the largest bulbs. The overall effect was that the air shimmered everywhere Conor looked, like he was peering through a fly's wings.

In the center of the city was an open hole leading into the earth, from which the warm air rose up to pass through the ceiling of the cavern. *It must warm the whole city*, Conor realized. It was certainly a welcome change after the chill of the tunnels.

More and more of the Sadreans emerged from hiding. As they did, they looked up at the newcomers and froze, astonishment slackening their faces. Conor heard gasps echo throughout the cavern. After letting her people gawk at them for a minute, Xanthe whistled and called out something in her language, waving them along. They didn't budge, though.

Conor felt his face flush as the dozens of Sadreans staring up became hundreds and then thousands. Right in front of his eyes a dignified woman holding the hands of two children fell to the ground and broke into sobs of joy. A large bat hung from a fold of the woman's shift—it seemed some Sadreans had spirit animals, too.

Down at the base of a mushroom tree, a Sadrean woman stood before a pen in which a number of fuzzy white spiders were crawling over themselves to eat the teeming beetles the woman poured from a bucket. She held it slackly as she stared in wonder at the outsiders, the insects flooding the floor of the pen.

Spiders as livestock. Conor shuddered.

Meilin opened her eyes, and seemed to be just as stunned by the sight of all these people paused in the middle of their everyday lives miles under the earth, staring up at *them*; her mouth hung slack and her hand curled around Conor's elbow in awe.

"*Phos Astos* means 'the city of light,'" Xanthe said, surveying her home as she gripped the netting. "Sadre has always protected Erdas from the Wyrm. We were the guardians you didn't even know you had. Now I fear this city is all that remains of us."

Takoda kept his face emotionless, but he cocked his head at Xanthe. "I'm sorry."

She laughed quietly, a light, silvery sound that ended sooner than Conor expected. "It isn't your fault."

"Does your family live in one of those homes carved out of the mushrooms?" Meilin asked.

"Yes," Xanthe said, her eyes going proudly to one of the smaller mushrooms on the city's edge. "In that one there. I will look forward to introducing you to them. But first you should meet the elders. Now that they know you're here, they'll assemble at our *teilidh*—our mural chamber. Come, follow me."

Without further preamble, Xanthe swung around the edge of the net and let go, dropping twenty feet or so until she hit the next one down. She let the rebound pitch her off the edge and drop her to the last net. Patting her hair flat in the pink light of the glowing city, she gracefully stepped off onto Phos Astos's stone floor.

Takoda was the first to the edge of their net, placing his hands in the same position Xanthe had. "How are you so comfortable with all this?" Conor asked.

"Cliff diving is a very popular hobby in Southern Nilo," Takoda said with a wink, before swan diving to the net below. He folded into a cannonball at the last moment and took a gigantic bounce to the next net down, hooting in glee the whole time. An admiring cheer rose from the watching Sadreans.

"Our man of mystery," Meilin said in amazement as she watched Takoda stride forward and introduce himself to the nearby Sadreans. "Shy with us and assertive with everyone else."

Conor held out his hand. "Here. Since you're scared of heights, do you want to go together?"

Meilin nodded, biting her lip, and gratefully took Conor's hand. "We'll wait until you're ready," Conor said.

She peered over the edge. "I—I don't know if I can do this, Conor," she stammered.

"Of course you can," he said, kneeling beside her on the swaying net. "Just—"

"Ha!" Meilin yelled, then with one expert movement pushed Conor over. He fell twenty feet, screaming his head off, belly flopping onto the net below. He lay still, hands over his face while he listened to the giggles of a few thousand watching Sadreans.

The net surged as Meilin landed beside him, chuckling. "I'm not afraid of heights, you dummy," she said.

"Are you pleased with yourself?" Conor asked, shaking his head.

"Yes, very," she said.

Reaching over, Conor slowly and deliberately placed a hand on Meilin's back and unceremoniously heaved her off the net.

By the time they'd stepped onto the city's rock floor, Conor and Meilin were breathless with laughter. That stopped quickly, though, once they saw that the assembled residents of Phos Astos were still staring at them.

"Come," Xanthe said as she began to weave a passage through the mushroom buildings. "The elders will be waiting."

When the Sadreans didn't move out of the way, she made a clicking noise in her throat and waved her hand to shoo them away. "I'm sorry," she said. "It must make you uncomfortable to have them ogling you like this."

Even though most of the Sadreans reluctantly returned to their business, as he hesitantly started forward Conor caught the eyes of no fewer than a dozen who were still staring at him. When they saw him looking back, the Sadreans startled and turned to other tasks, pretending they hadn't been gaping. Conor watched them with interest as he passed. Some were sharpening spears made from resin, or swords fashioned from crystals. Others were slivering a large black mushroom, separating wafer-thin layers that another Sadrean was sewing into patchwork cloth. Entranced, Conor realized with a start that his friends were already a dozen paces ahead.

"The reason Phos Astos has been able to hold out against the Many for this long," Xanthe was explaining to Meilin as Conor caught up, "is that our city is surrounded by a plain of flat glacier stone that extends half a mile wide and is as smooth as a mushroom. Once, a black river passed over it, and we had to raft across to reach this cavern. But now we've discovered how to dam the river and walk across the dry riverbed. The Many may be powerful, but when they become infected, they lose their memory and their reason. When they attack, they surge across the plain without any caution, filling it like the black river once did."

They lose their memory and their reason. The words rattled around Conor's head.

"And that's when you release the dam!" Meilin said.

Xanthe shrugged humbly. "It has worked in the past. But it's not a perfect system. The pressure of the water is strong enough that it takes us days to muscle the mechanisms back into place and drain the trap, leaving us vulnerable in the meantime. And we only have one shot— we have to time the flooding perfectly when the Many are all on the plain itself. If we miss any, then they can still get across after the initial flood sweeps the others away."

"Still," Meilin said, shaking her head in admiration and stepping around a Sadrean child with his thumb in his mouth, staring up at her in awe. "It's a stroke of genius. I'm impressed."

"Thank you," Xanthe said, clearly pleased with herself.

The tunnel sloped downward, and to continue along it they had to turn sideways, pressing the edges of their boots sharply into the rock. Xanthe kept cutting backward glances, obviously still fascinated by the outsiders. In one of her distracted moments, she tumbled—and it was Takoda who caught her. He flashed out one hand and ably grabbed hold of her shoulder, righting her without losing his own balance. Xanthe smiled shyly and thanked him.

As he walked, Conor turned Xanthe's words over in his mind. Maybe the Many weren't as mindless as everyone was assuming—which meant they were more dangerous than anyone thought.

"Careful, now," Xanthe said. "We're approaching the dam's mechanism."

The slate all around them began to shine as Conor's torch streaked light along its surface. The tunnel sloped down before giving out onto a black plain. They were at a ledge ten feet or so above it, at the top of the dam. The mechanism to open it was simple: Thick bands of corded rope were wrapped around two great wheels of iron, with handles evenly spaced along each.

"These wheels connect to a large door damming the river upstream," Xanthe said. "By turning them, we can control the amount of water flowing out."

"And wash out the Many," Conor said.

"Underground locks must have been difficult to build," Meilin said approvingly.

Xanthe held her finger up to her lips to quiet them, then paused, her head tilted in the air. Then she shook her head. "I thought I heard something," she said. "But it's nothing."

She knelt at the ledge's lip. A small mushroom was growing there, gold in color and shaped like a bell. And, like a bell, it rang out when Xanthe flicked it. "These are what we call screamers," she said proudly. "We've cultivated them over the centuries as a warning system. If the Many approach us, they'll have to cross through tracts of these. The mushrooms set off a chain reaction all the way into Phos Astos, ringing so loudly that they wake everyone up. Come, this way."

Xanthe made a quick turn, disappearing into an opening in the slate wall. Remembering the tight tunnels they'd been in when the jabbering horde had attacked, Conor quailed. But after watching Meilin and Takoda calmly enter the passageway, he followed, too.

The glowing pink-and-green dust was back, coating the walkway. Conor watched, transfixed, as it swirled around the ankles of his companions, whose paces left foot-sized patches of clear slate behind them.

"You're really in for a treat," Xanthe said. "I love these murals."

"Shouldn't someone be keeping an eye on the riverbed?" Conor asked. "Just to be safe?"

"The screamers won't fail," the girl replied surely. "And the elders are waiting for us in the mural chamber. They're going to be so excited to meet you."

They stepped into a cavern, only a dozen feet across but so tall that Conor couldn't see its roof. Mushrooms grew up and down the walls, a soft carpet of glowing plants. It all served as illumination for the masterpiece in the room's center.

A massive stalagmite had built up there, extending halfway up the vaulting room. Carvings were chipped into its surface, images winding around and up the thick structure. The first looked like a snake swimming in an ocean of stars. Conor leaned forward to examine it, only then noticing that there were people quietly assembled around the far side.

Conor eased around to see a half dozen Sadrean men and women standing around the stalagmite in a perfect semicircle, clad in voluminous robes made from the same shimmering black cloth as Xanthe's shift. They'd been talking to one another in hushed voices, but jolted to attention at the new arrivals.

"Here are the upsiders!" Xanthe exclaimed to them. "Conor, Meilin, and Takoda, these are the elders of Phos Astos."

As one, the elders stared at them with something like awe on their faces. Conor flushed with embarrassment.

"Thanks be to you," said one elderly woman, her joints creaking as she got down to one knee, tears in her eyes. "Our saviors have finally come."

A second elder dropped to his knees, tears streaming down his wrinkled face.

The companions stared at one another. "No, please, no one else get on their knees," Conor said.

The tallest elder stepped toward them. He was a handsome, severe-looking man with a patch over one eye. "My name is Ingailor. Takoda, Conor, and Meilin, please know how honored we are that you have come. This moment has been prophesied for a long time. You've been called to us to defeat the Wyrm."

"I'm sorry," Takoda said. "But could someone tell me what this Wyrm is that everyone keeps talking about?"

All the elders went perfectly still. The old woman who had been kneeling staggered to her feet, confusion slackening her face.

Ingailor shook his head. "I don't understand. Do you have another name for the Wyrm up on the surface?"

"Maybe," Takoda said. "I don't know." He looked to Meilin. *Can you give me some help here?*

She shook her head.

Xanthe grabbed Conor's shoulder. When he turned toward her, he was startled to see hope in her eyes that was so desperate it looked almost like panic. "What about the weapon?" she asked.

Conor met her wide eyes. "I'm sorry, Xanthe. I don't know what you're talking about."

One of the elders gave an anguished cry and dropped to the ground.

Ingailor kept his face impassive. "If you don't have the weapon, why have you come here?"

"The Evertree is sick," Conor explained. "And the source of its illness is coming from below."

Xanthe stepped in front of the companions, and addressed the elders. "I'm sorry! They know nothing of us," she said. "But fate must have brought them here to save us from the Many. It's too much of a coincidence not to be ordained."

Ingailor raised a hand to stop Xanthe from speaking further, the expression on his face both tough and oddly gentle. The rest of the elders weren't as good at hiding their feelings—they were clearly aghast. "I don't doubt that you believe this. But I'm not sure what these children can do that we haven't already tried. And without the weapon . . ."

"I understand that you must be disappointed," Xanthe said, keeping her eyes downcast. "But perhaps if we show them the story in the murals, they might still see something in them that we haven't."

Ingailor smiled wanly. In that moment, Conor realized that he was only being brave for his people—he had given up all hope. "That's a good plan. You do your family proud. And we have nothing to lose." He turned to the rest of the assembled elders. *"Belsharth roha."*

"Belsharth rohi," they said back, nodding. Then, as one, they parted and shuffled gloomily out of the cavern.

As Ingailor stepped to one of the carvings, Xanthe stayed close to his side. Conor heard her whisper: "Trust my intuition in this. All hope is not lost, Elder Ingailor."

Ingailor didn't react, and instead pointed to the image carved in the wall above him. It was of a dozen men and women in a primitive boat crossing a choppy sea, their rows of oars dipping into the water.

"This shows the founding of Erdas," he explained. "The bands of hunters that came together to become the civilization known as the Hellans."

Meilin's eyes widened in surprise. "I've read about the Hellans," she said. "They were some of the earliest astronomers. Many of their constellations are still used in navigation today."

It was Xanthe who pointed to the next carved image, a giant tree surrounded by the shapes of fifteen animals— each icon representing one of the Great Beasts. Conor was pleased to see that Briggan and Jhi and Uraza were pictured near one another, friends even way back then. That was only half the image, however: The tree's roots extended down deep, wrapping around what looked like an egg, which the artist had crusted with the dust of sapphires and emeralds. It looked like the tree was cradling the egg in the lattice of its roots—or caging it.

"This is the essential conflict of Erdas and Sadre," Xanthe said. "The Evertree versus the Wyrm. The tree provides life. It bonds animals and humans as allies. The Wyrm is . . . something else. We suspect it may be as old as the Evertree itself. It has always slept deep in the earth, contained within its roots."

"The Wyrm is a parasite," Ingailor said with sudden vehemence, touching his fingers to the egg in the carving. "It is chaos and hunger incarnate. For a millennium it has slept, encased in an egg kept dormant by the power of the Evertree. But it was a restless sleep."

"How do you know all this?" Meilin asked. "The Evertree was hidden from humans until very recently."

"The wisest of the Great Beasts sought out the Hellans," Ingailor said, pulling his hand away from the jeweled egg. "Though the Great Beasts came from the Evertree, only *he* sensed the rot that lurked beneath it. He told the Hellans about the danger of the Wyrm and gave us our task: By making sure the Evertree's roots were healthy and strong, we could help delay the eventual coming of the Wyrm. The Hellans above were tasked with building a weapon, something capable of stopping the Wyrm if it ever broke free."

Conor's heart sank. Just a small piece of a single parasite was slowly taking his body from him. Without the weapon, what chance did they have against the Wyrm and all of its minions?

Meilin stood close to Conor, tension radiating from her.

They moved to the next panel. There, Hellans hugged good-bye, tears on their faces, as half of them climbed down into a cave. "The Hellans divided into two people," said Xanthe. "Our brothers and sisters stayed above. We, the Sadreans, went below to tend to the Evertree's roots. That was the last time we ever lived on the surface."

"Not too long ago," Ingailor continued, "the Evertree's roots withered, and the Wyrm's egg dropped. Then, just as mysteriously, new roots began to grow where the old had been. They cradled the egg again, but they were young yet, and much weaker than before. The Wyrm sensed that weakness. It is waking. Worse still, the fall cracked the egg, allowing small gray parasites, extensions of the Wyrm's will, to spill out. They have spread all through Sadre, sowing chaos and possessing our people."

"The Many," Conor said, goose bumps breaking out along his arms. Maybe it was only his imagination, but he thought he could sense his own parasite twitching.

"This also explains why the Evertree is sick," Takoda said.

"Worse than sick," said Xanthe. "Dying! As the Wyrm wakes, it consumes the tree for its power."

"The parasites are on the surface, too," Conor said, fingers clenched on his arm. "A man named Zerif is using them to possess the Great Beasts—and people. Maybe we can seal the egg somehow." Even if it was too late for him, he could possibly help to save others from the infection that was claiming him. "Can you lead us there?"

"The path to the Wyrm's egg is crawling with the Many. Any who attempted that journey would not return." Ingailor frowned wearily. "I'm sorry, but Phos Astos needs its elders now more than ever. I must stay here."

"But I am in my wander years," Xanthe said. "I've been to the Evertree's roots before. That was before the Many began their assault, but I know the way. Let me be the one who brings the upsiders to the Wyrm."

"Before you go offering yourself up for risks like that," Meilin said, "you should know that we don't even have a plan for what we'll do about the Wyrm once we get there. The Hellan civilization is ancient history. If they had a weapon, it most likely disappeared with them."

Xanthe clenched her fists and raised her head, a new resolve in her expression. "I had hoped that you might be the Hellans. I let myself believe you had brought us their weapon, and I know now that I was wrong. But I won't let go of my belief that you'll save us. That *will* happen."

"Xanthe's right. It won't help any of us to give up hope—" Takoda started, but froze.

A shrill, thunderous ringing filled the chamber. The sound was powerful enough to shake multicolored motes down from the walls, bathing the air in color.

Xanthe and Ingailor were instantly in motion, sprinting out of the cavern. "The screamers!" Xanthe called over her shoulder. "The Many are attacking!"

As they sped down the tunnel leading back to the plain, the mushroom dust swirled up in great gusts, clouding Conor's vision and making him cough. He covered his mouth with his sleeve as they dashed down the sloping tunnel.

The companions skidded to a stop just shy of the ledge at the tunnel's exit. They were only ten feet or so above the smooth slate plain, two wheels and a lock the only things guarding them—and Phos Astos—from annihilation.

Xanthe lay her hand over the screamer's bulby head until it stilled, then she and Ingailor hunched over one of the wheels, talking heatedly in their language.

"When's the last time you used this thing?" Conor asked.

Ingailor spared one glance at Conor before returning to examining the wheel. "We've never had a second attack come this soon—we've only just finished the repairs from the last wave. The guards are on their way, but we'll need your help in the meantime."

"Of course," Meilin said.

Xanthe measured up their group. "Conor, Takoda, and I will take one wheel. Meilin can help you, Ingailor. That should be enough strength on both sides to do it. Once the guards arrive, they can take over."

Xanthe sifted through a pouch at her waist. Her hand came out with a small glowing pink globe, no bigger than a marble. Standing at the lip of the tunnel opening, she lanced it as high as she could over the slate plain.

It lit the glossy stone below like soft fire, casting a pink glow that brought out constellations of glittery highlights within the rock.

Revealing the Many.

A few dozen of the monsters were halfway across. They'd been creeping toward them in the darkness, but in the shock of the sudden light they staggered, reeling back and gasping. Before Conor's eyes, he saw them scrunch their eyelids shut and press forward, crawling on all fours, shockingly fast.

He imagined those creatures—the kind of creature *he* would become once the parasite got to his forehead—lurching forward, hunting them, their long-nailed hands groping through the darkness. His body broke into shudders, and he couldn't make it stop.

"Release it!" he gasped. "Release the water!"

"Stay calm!" Ingailor commanded. "It will take the Many a few more minutes to cross the plain. The bulk of the horde is behind them, and we need to catch as many as possible in our trap."

In an attempt to calm himself, Conor imagined the most peaceful thing he could: his old herd. He pictured the sheep's soft curly fur, smelled the wet musty scent of their skin, listened to their soft bleats as they chewed grass. It was enough of a distraction to keep the terror at bay—almost. Then Xanthe threw another one of her stones and illuminated the plain again. Conor's sheep vanished from his mind for good.

The plain was swarming with the Many—at least a thousand of them, staggering and lurching across the smooth, glittering surface, crawling over one another in their unthinking haste. They all froze for a moment under the brilliant light, then it faded and Conor was blind again. He closed his eyes, biting back his terror, and flailed in the darkness until he contacted one of the wheel's handles. He almost started turning it on his own, but stopped himself just in time, instead grinding his palms into his wheel. *Just let us release the dam!* he silently pleaded.

The nearest of the Many hadn't been more than twenty feet away, and they were moving fast.

"Hold . . . hold . . . and *now!*" Ingailor cried. "The wheels!"

Gasping in relief, Conor began to turn his handle. With Xanthe and Takoda straining beside him, the wheel began to shift. From a few feet away, he could hear Meilin and Ingailor's wheel groan and shudder as it, too, lurched into motion.

"It's working!" he heard Meilin exclaim.

Which was when Conor's wheel stopped.

"Is it supposed to do this?" Takoda asked.

"No!" Xanthe said frantically. "It's jammed. It's jammed!"

They heaved, but the wheel gave only an inch or two before springing back to its original position.

"Ingailor!" Xanthe shrieked.

Conor could hear the Many right under their ledge: the sound of their fingernails scratching against the stone, their grunts and moans as they tried to scramble up to get them. Conor imagined they'd mound up soon, start to climb one another . . . and then they'd be upon them, and all would be lost.

Conor tugged frantically, but the wheel was still stuck.

"Xanthe?" Ingailor called over, concerned. "What's happening? The gate's not opening!"

"I have to do it," Takoda said.

"What do you mean?" Xanthe asked, perplexed.

But Conor knew precisely what Takoda meant. There was a radiant flash and a popping sound, then a heavy weight hit the ground beside him.

"What the−?" Xanthe said, shocked.

Conor heard a familiar grunt, and then Kovo was beside him, the gorilla's coarse hair bristling against Conor's arm as he took a place at the wheel. Conor felt a rough hand over his own and realized the ape wanted his handle, too. He leaped out of the way. Startled, Xanthe tumbled beside him.

"You have a spirit animal?" she asked.

"It's . . . more like he has me," Takoda said ruefully. "But yes."

With a scream of metal, their wheel began to turn. Kovo grunted as he slapped the handles, getting up more and more speed until they were whizzing past.

"It's working! It's open!" Ingailor called.

Kovo seemed to be enjoying himself. He continued to pelt the wheel, pushing it faster and faster.

"Hey!" Takoda said sternly. "Stop now."

The ape roared in anger at Takoda, baring his sharp teeth.

"*Please*," said Takoda. Before the boy's pleading eyes, the anger drained out of Kovo.

"Listen!" Xanthe said excitedly. Her eyes had been on the plain ever since their wheel started turning. "Water!"

Conor heard the rushing sound, too.

So did the Many. They began to scream, an awful, high-pitched sound.

Xanthe took another stone from her pouch, this one a pale green color, wider and flatter than the previous. She hurled it to the ceiling of the cavern, where it struck and splattered, green goo softly illuminating the scene below.

The light came just in time to reveal an enormous wave of black water as it struck. It had such force behind it that the first rows of the Many disappeared entirely, swept deep into the dark, surging tide. More and more fell beneath it, their screams cutting off short as the water swept across the plain, bowling over ghoulish white bodies and dragging them under.

Conor watched the trap do its deadly work. Once the water began to slow into a swift current without any whitecaps, he could see that none of the Many remained. The sudden black river had seized them all.

"Where did they *go*?" Conor asked. He'd expected to feel joy at seeing the monsters swept away. Instead, the gaping emptiness of the plain stood as a painful reminder of his own plight. Though they called them monsters now, the Many had once been people, just like him.

"Rivers run throughout Sadre," Xanthe said grimly. "The tunnels we use are all old riverbeds. This water will flow in a thousand different directions, into the deepest parts of the earth. That's where the Many have been dragged. Those who haven't drowned are lost forever."

"Will any survive?" Meilin asked.

"It's unlikely," Xanthe said, staring back across the plain. "Though we've never swept quite this many down before."

"It's so sad," Conor said.

Meilin squeezed his arm.

"Ingailor, I'll put out a call for workers to come set the trap again," Xanthe said.

There was no answer.

"Ingailor?" Xanthe turned around and gasped.

Ingailor's pink eyes were wide, his hands held in shock over his chest. Once Xanthe saw what he was looking at, she took a step back in surprise.

They were staring at Kovo. Illuminated by the soft green light from above, the ape looked especially fearsome. The tips of his jet-black hair were lit by faerie fire, broadening his already massive physique. He stood on all fours, taking them all in. The expression in his scarlet eyes was inscrutable, but the one thing about Kovo that was unmistakable, ever unmistakable, was his brutal intelligence.

"So . . . I guess I should tell you that we have spirit animals," Conor said. "This is Takoda's."

Xanthe stared forward, her voice softened by awe, her eyes shining. "Is this who I think it is?"

"Oh, you recognize him?" Meilin asked with a nervous sigh. "The Great Beasts of Erdas died and have been reborn as spirit animals. That's what caused the Evertree's roots to regrow six months ago. Conor, Takoda, and I *all* summoned Great Beasts. So you don't have to be afraid of Kovo . . . probably."

"You don't understand my question," Xanthe said, turning her shocked eyes on Meilin.

"I think I *do* understand," Takoda said, shaking his head. "When you told us the origin of Sadre, you said that the wisest of the Great Beasts taught the Hellans about the Wyrm. We assumed you were talking about Tellun . . . but you weren't, were you?"

Xanthe shook her head, staring reverently at the ape. When she spoke, it was directly to him. "No. The one who was trying to save the world was Kovo. It was you."

NORTH, SOUTH, WEST

THE TRIBE OFFERED ABEKE AND ROLLAN HORSES TO ride. Rollan thought nothing of it—Greenhaven had three stables full of them, so giving up a horse or two seemed like no big deal—but Abeke bowed low and thanked them effusively.

"Giving up a work animal is a tremendous sacrifice for a nomad tribe," she explained as she adjusted her horse's saddle pads and shortened its stirrups. "They must have spent years traveling with these horses, raising them from colts."

Aynar had mapped them a trail that would lead back to the *Tellun's Pride II* over paths solid enough for the horses. They'd follow the swath of muddied grass the yak herd had left behind, head due east along a valley between two mountains, and cross an open plain to the pier where their ship was moored. Sticking to terrain suitable for horses meant traveling a longer distance, but with mounts they should be back by the end of the day.

"I'm relieved we have a new way to go," Abeke said. "If Zerif is tailing us, it's safest to press forward and not loop back."

Anda watched patiently as his new companions mounted up. Tellun wasn't a particularly demonstrative elk, but he did stand very close to the boy, his broad chest right behind Anda's shoulders. Whenever he leaned back and scratched through Tellun's white and gold fur, the elk scrunched his eyes in stoic pleasure.

Rollan shook his head, mystified. "Anda is scratching the *leader of the Great Beasts.*"

"Not just scratching him," Abeke said as she mounted her horse.

"What do you mean?" Rollan asked.

"Did you notice how many horses there are? And how many riders?"

Rollan's jaw dropped open. "Wait. You don't mean—"

And then it happened. Anda elegantly wrapped his long arms around Tellun's neck and launched from the earth, swinging around to land neatly on the Great Elk's back.

"You do realize *who* you're riding, right?" Rollan asked out of the side of his mouth.

"Yes," Anda said, smiling. "My friend!"

"And you're fine with this?" Rollan asked Tellun, shaking his head.

"Why not?" Abeke said. "*We* rode him to the Evertree."

"That was different," Rollan sniffed.

In reply, the elk raised his antlers haughtily into the air and bounded down the beaten path. Anda threw his arms around his neck to hold on.

"At least Anda didn't put a saddle on him," Rollan grumbled as he kicked his own horse into motion. "That would have been simply too much."

Sure, Rollan figured, the tribe might have made a big sacrifice by offering them two horses, but they'd clearly been strategic about *which* two horses they gave up. Rollan's had the approximate speed and power of a bread box. Abeke's kept slobbering everywhere, and tried to throw her twice within the first fifty paces. Though an elk was by no means a traditional mount for any human, it was soon clear that Anda would be making far better time than Rollan and Abeke. "Say hi to everyone at Greenhaven for us!" Rollan called as the boy pulled farther and farther ahead.

Essix didn't seem to know what to do with herself. At first, with millennia-honed instinct, she forgot about Rollan entirely and flew above Tellun instead. Then, after about an hour of travel, she returned to Rollan's side. She made a piercing, confused cry, her eyes darting around. She took off back toward Tellun, then thought better of it and returned to Rollan, then took off again and returned to Tellun, soon returning to Rollan's side.

"I know," Rollan told her. "It's confusing to me, too. It's Tellun, but he's not using his boomy voice."

Uraza seemed to be taking everything in stride—but then again, the leopard had never been one to lose her cool. She loped along beside Abeke's persnickety horse, low to the ground, frequently stopping to sniff the air or the base of a tree.

"There must be new smells around here for our kitty cat," Rollan said to Abeke, trying to kick some extra speed from his horse as it tiptoed along the ground. At this rate, it would be winter before they made it to the boat.

"It's not that," Abeke said with a worried expression. "Her nose is many times more sensitive than ours. I think she's detecting something amiss."

Uraza paused and looked up at Rollan with her wide lavender eyes, as if to say, *See? Show a little more respect.*

"Which direction?" Rollan asked.

Uraza flicked her gaze north. Rollan pivoted in his saddle to look that way. All he could see were the white-capped cliffs of distant mountains, skirted by a broad, flat plain and isolated clumps of desperate pines. A small plume of dust was at the horizon, but that could have been caused by any number of things. "Well, good thing we're heading east and not north, then," Rollan said.

They continued, following the distant blip of Anda and Tellun as boy and elk easily picked their way over rocky terrain.

Rollan decided it was time for a better view. He scanned the sky for Essix, then began to focus on her shape. Nothing happened for a long moment, then suddenly the world pitched and the ground fell away. Rollan felt momentarily sick—no amount of practice had ever helped that—but soon he was able to see the world through Essix's eyes. The falcon felt him enter her mind and churred companionably.

At first Rollan used Essix's high vantage point to look

north, but he couldn't see anything out of the ordinary, couldn't tell what Uraza might be smelling.

West was another story.

When Rollan followed Essix's vision around the plains, he came up with nothing the first few times. But then he heard Essix shriek, and grew alert. With her telescopic vision, Essix zeroed in on an abandoned campsite. Whoever had left it behind had been careful to cover their tracks—the surrounding ground was smoothed over, and the blackened stones of the fire pit had been scattered. But there was still the faintest burning ember in one of the fire logs, trailing up a whisper of smoke. Vision less acute than Essix's would have missed it.

Rollan returned his consciousness to his own body with a dizzying lurch, and called out to Abeke to hold up. At the same time, he saw that Anda and Tellun were making their way back to them. They met under the shelter of a broad, leafy tree. Rollan's thoughts flicked to the ailing Evertree, and he realized that even this brief moment of relief after finding Tellun might have been too much of an indulgence.

Anda and Tellun were wearing concerned expressions even before Abeke told them that Uraza had scented intruders to the north. When Rollan added that Essix had spotted an abandoned campfire to the west, Anda gave a grim smile. "Tellun is upset as well. But he keeps looking to the south."

"We can't all be correct," Abeke said.

"We'd best hope that we're not all correct," Rollan said. "Otherwise, we're nearly surrounded."

"I'm not a ranger," Anda said. "But I can only think that this doesn't change our plan. We're heading through that valley to the east. So far, that's also the only direction where we haven't sensed any danger."

"I agree," Abeke said. "And let's have our wits about us as we go."

"Being especially alert, of course, to anything that might be approaching from the *west*," Rollan said.

He watched Abeke try—and fail—to hide her smile. "By west, I think you meant north," she said.

"Or rather south," Anda said, smiling as well. Then his expression grew serious. "Regardless of the direction of the threat, Tellun and I won't scout ahead anymore. We should stay close, to defend one another."

They started moving again. To the east appeared two large mountains flanking a narrow valley, just as Aynar had told them. Anda and Abeke picked up their pace, but Rollan immediately felt himself falling behind. His horse was simply too old and too ornery to keep up with the others. Abeke and Anda stopped to wait for him after a few minutes, and when Rollan reached them, Anda laid his hand on Tellun's forehead, right between the antlers. The two communed for a moment, and then Rollan's mount whickered. The tension drained out of the horse's body, and when Anda and Tellun took off again, Rollan's horse followed perkily, as spry as a colt.

Rollan didn't even need to hold on to the reins, his horse had become that sure and graceful. "What just happened?" he called to Anda.

"I'm . . . not totally sure," Anda said. "I have only

inklings of Tellun's skill so far. We haven't been together for long. But I think he can communicate freely with any animal he meets."

Abeke pulled up alongside them. "You're well paired. You were the listener of your tribe, and Tellun has served a similar role for the Great Beasts. He has always been a quiet leader."

Anda stroked Tellun's long neck as he rode. "It's nice to feel understood."

Abeke pulled her hair behind her so she could see forward better. "You know, my father always wanted me to be pretty and refined, like my sister Soama. But that wasn't who I was: I was a hunter. I preferred the solitude of the plains, with my bow in hand."

A flicker of pain passed over Anda's features. "My father wished for a hunter. But he got me. I can hunt mushrooms and healing herbs, but that's about the extent of it."

"It can take time," Abeke said. "But he'll come around. You summoned Tellun. Your story will become one of your people's legends. My father and I only started to understand each other recently, but our love was there all along."

"I miss my tribe already," Anda said simply. "I miss them very much."

As they neared the twin mountains, they left the herd's beaten trail entirely and picked their way through scrabbly brush. Though Rollan's horse was no longer resistant and cranky, it did start to slow from sheer exhaustion. She dropped her neck and stumbled, a sure sign the mare was nearing her limits. At one point, Anda called the group to a stop.

"I hate to say it, but I think we should camp and find the ship in the morning," Anda said.

Rollan nodded gratefully.

"Why?" Abeke asked. "There's still plenty of daylight."

"Look how high the mountains rise on either side of the valley where we must pass," Anda said. "Once we're in the canyon between them, they'll block out any light that isn't directly overhead. The sun will set hours early in that valley. We'll be in the dark, with only two access points. If we're attacked, we could easily be overwhelmed."

"Oh," Abeke said. "I hadn't considered that."

"We'll have to camp one night," Rollan said. "It'll be cold, but it's best not to make a campfire. An attack could easily come from the west."

"Or north," Abeke said.

"Or south," Anda said.

"Let's hope none of us are right," Rollan said.

"We've assigned night watches before," Abeke said. "And we've handled anything that came at us."

"That may be true," Anda said, "but we have a saying, *oranu yeno simula oranu mordico*. 'A confident plainsman is a dead plainsman.' Let's camp once we reach the base of the mountains. I'll feel safer with a cliff face at our backs."

Rollan hated the idea of being without good shelter at night in the whispering plains. All the same, he was glad they had decided not to press forward. The prospect of navigating a night-dark alley between steep, foreboding mountains was none too appealing.

Though it was afternoon, once the cliff blocked the sunlight, the chill of twilight entered their bones. As they assembled their bedrolls and made camp, Uraza was the first to start shivering. Abeke called the leopard into passive state so the tropical cat wouldn't suffer. Essix had techniques to keep herself warm, though the normally regal gyrfalcon did look a trifle silly with her feathers puffed out, more like a ruffled chicken than a bird of prey. Tellun and Anda were the only ones who seemed fully at ease, standing on the rocky ground and staring out watchfully.

After a simple cold meal of seeds and greens, they settled in for the night. Once Tellun had chosen a position and lay down, it was impossible to resist putting their bedrolls alongside him to warm themselves against his fur. Rollan felt a little scandalous, using the greatest of the Great Beasts for his body heat.

"Do you think you'll be able to fall asleep, Rollan?" Anda asked while they stretched out on their backs. The first stars were twinkling in the slate sky.

"Hmm whaa . . . ?" Rollan asked. Anda's question had caught him mid-yawn.

"You go to sleep if you can. I'll take first watch. I'd like to replace Abeke's neck dressings, anyway. Then I'll switch off to her, and you can take the last watch."

"Sounds just fi-iine to me," Rollan said around another yawn. "How's your neck doing, by the way?"

"Much better," Abeke said. Rollan could hear the smile in her voice. "Thanks to Anda."

"Yes, thanks to Anda," Rollan said. "And we should all thank Tellun, for being so very snuggly." Rollan wriggled his hands under the elk's warm body, and the greatest of the Great Beasts snorted in response.

Despite the cold, Rollan slept deeply. He dreamed of Arctica, of balancing on an ice floe with Meilin, giggling as it tilted, trying to keep their balance as each jostled the other. Jhi and Essix were on two more floes nearby, bobbing in a frigid sea, watching. It only slowly dawned on Rollan that they were strangely impassive, even as Rollan and Meilin were having the time of their lives.

Come on, Essix, Rollan thought in the dream. *Lighten up!*

Dream-Essix looked at him like a stranger. Then she opened her mouth, and rolls of black rot came streaming out. It flooded her floe, tipping the bird into the icy depths. Then Jhi was retching black rot, too, and Meilin was screaming and tipping in.

Then—slam—the dream was over. Rollan was suddenly awake and gasping, hands patting the cord of rope that tied his pants, groggily searching for his dagger sheath. The dream was over, but a very real pain was wracking his body. His insides felt like they'd wrapped around a giant's fist, then yanked out of his body.

"What happened?" came a startled voice. Anda.

"I don't know," Rollan managed to say. Then, before he could say anything more, it happened again. The giant yanked his insides to the horizon and let them snap back. He rolled onto his side, face contorted in pain. "Argh!"

Now that he was awake for it, Rollan heard Anda scream, and Abeke, too. "Rollan, what's happening?" she cried.

"I don't know," he gasped.

But then he did. He recognized this awful pain. Rollan had felt it once before, under a bloodred sky at the end of the world. "Our spirit animal bonds!" he shouted. "They're breakin—*ahh*!"

Once more, his guts wrenched.

"I don't understand," Anda said, his voice unsteady with fear. "Why is this happening to us?"

Rollan sat up, hugging his arms around his torso for comfort while he waited for the next tremor.

They breathed in silence in the darkness, waiting for the next wave of the pain. But it didn't come.

"Our bonds are under attack," Abeke said to Anda, her breathing slowly returning to normal. "I think . . . I think it's because the Evertree is sick."

"It—it was horrible," Anda stammered in the near darkness. "Like something was punching my spine."

"Essix?" Rollan called, remembering his dream. Though he could see the outline of the falcon nearby in the dim light, for once he didn't have an inherent sense of where she was. It was a bleak and empty feeling, like grief.

Then the fluffy cold-weather version of Essix edged over to Rollan and snuggled in close. Gradually, as if it had been frozen in a block of ice that was slowly melting,

Rollan's link to Essix was returning. But it still felt like a small, frailer version of what it once was.

"Abeke . . ." Rollan said. "Something's changed."

"I feel it, too," she said grimly. "My link to Uraza feels . . . cold."

"I think it might be coming back to me and Essix, slowly. Maybe we'll be okay in the morning."

Anda reached his arms around Tellun, his eyes closed tight. "I can't tell," he murmured.

"There's nothing we can do now," Abeke said. "I'll summon Uraza in the morning and see where things stand."

"You're right," Rollan said, nodding. "Get some rest." Then he turned to Anda. "I'll take my watch now."

"Wake us at the first sign of danger," Abeke whispered.

They must have been truly exhausted; neither Anda nor Abeke put up a fight, and were soon huddled into themselves, out cold.

Normally Rollan found it hard to stay awake when he was on watch, but there would be no trouble with that tonight. He sat up, rigid with worry, and listened to the noises of the Amayan night. Hugging his knees close, he scanned the near dark and listened to frogs, insects, and the first warm-ups of morning songbirds. One was particularly insistent, and was soon met by another answering call from far off.

Probably two birds falling in love from afar, Rollan thought grumpily. *At least* they're *happy. I'm just cold. And worried.*

His thoughts went to Meilin. Essix hadn't been the only spirit animal in his dream—wherever she was, had Meilin felt a similar rupture to her bond with Jhi? He hoped she was more comfortable tonight than he was, sleepless in this chilly air and waiting for danger to strike. Had she and Conor found the mysterious door? He wished that they could all be together, camping with Tellun.

But Meilin wasn't there, so Rollan would have to spend his watch with only Essix for company. At least the falcon was sticking close—she probably felt as confused as he did by the near loss of their bond. He stared out into the blackness, taking comfort from the slow rise and fall of his friends' breathing and Essix's little chirps. The falcon readjusted herself on Rollan's arm, fluffing and unfluffing her feathers, trying to find the right temperature.

"Are we okay?" Rollan whispered to the falcon. But though he could make a guess, he had no idea what she was feeling. He could only pray the connection returned soon.

Throughout it all, the songbirds continued their happy chirping. There were three of them now, Rollan realized. One from the north, one from the south, and one . . . from the west.

Filling with dread, Rollan rose quietly to his feet and unsheathed his dagger. He could see from the silvered outline of the twin mountains that the sun had dawned on the other side, but their massive forms were still blocking most of the light.

He was nervous but wasn't sure if he needed to awaken Abeke and Anda yet.

"Essix," Rollan whispered, "can you see enough to scout around?"

Before he had even finished asking, Essix took to the air, rising into the night as silent as a whisper.

Rollan held still and opened his senses as much as he could. The songbirds were coming closer. Songbirds in the night? Closing in from three directions?

His intuition set off alarms. "Anda, Abeke!" he hissed. "Get up!"

Whatever was hunting him must have been waiting for him to make a noise, because the moment Rollan spoke was the moment the first animal struck, from out of nowhere. Something sharp locked on Rollan's hamstring. He couldn't see enough to know what it was that had attacked him, but it was strong enough to yank him to the ground. Rollan flailed, trying to get back to his feet even as his attacker bit deeper and pulled.

A man shouted, with a voice Rollan recognized but couldn't quite place, and then the clearing was suddenly full of noise as attackers closed in. They came not from the west, the north, or the south.

They came from all three.

13

VICTORY

T HE GROUP WAS GRIPPED BY A QUEASY SILENCE ALL THE way back to Phos Astos. Unbidden, Meilin's mind kept replaying the sight of those white bodies struggling to get above frothing black water, inevitably failing and being swept under. She shivered. Carried off into the watery depths—it was a horrific way to go. Despite herself, she hoped at least a few of the monstrous creatures had some-how survived.

When the tunnel started to glow pink-green, Meilin knew they were nearing Phos Astos. Then they emerged into the main cavern, and she was again struck by the beauty of the lively oasis, glowing warmly in the midst of so many tons of dark and impenetrable rock. The nervous chatter of the Sadreans carried down the ruddy light of the entrance tunnel. Once she and the others had stepped out into the full light of the city, Meilin saw a ripple pass through them as they remarked on the strangers' return. The Sadreans paused in their tasks, became still and watchful, waiting for news.

Ingailor raised a hand to the watching crowd. "You can return to your duties," he said. "The Many attacked, but they have been fought off." There was no cheering, only grim nods, rustling, and murmurs as everyone returned to work. Fighting off the Many was clearly something that had happened often before. Even so, most looked up every few seconds to scan their surroundings as they returned to work.

The last to emerge from the tunnel was Takoda—with Kovo. The moment the gorilla clambered down the handholds in the stone wall and thudded to the cave floor, the cavern of Phos Astos filled with audible gasps. Men and women fell to their knees where they were, bowing their foreheads to the ground in reverence. A complicated and almost wistful expression on his face, Kovo grunted and paced, finally working his way to the center of the cavern. There, he stood up on two legs and slowly pivoted, taking in the sight of the people he had tasked eons ago to found their underground civilization. He roared.

The youngest of the Sadreans screamed, their shrieks joining the gorilla's roar and reverberating through the walls. The echoes strengthened one another until the noise sounded more like the rumbling of the earth than animal cries. Then the gorilla stopped, and gradually the cavern grew quiet.

Most of the Sadreans stood where they were along the edges of the giant mushrooms, but then the elders from the mural room made their way to the floor, expertly clambering down the handholds carved into the fiber. When they arrived, they formed a semicircle around the group.

One by one, the elders knelt, while Kovo lowered himself to the rock floor. One of the elders ran her hand over the shimmering fungus on the ground, then tentatively brought it toward the mighty ape. Meilin expected to see him bare his teeth, but Kovo stared into the distance coolly as the woman traced five lines across his cheek. Then the woman took another handful of color and traced it over her own cheek.

Each of the elders came forward and did the same, choosing a different part of Kovo to honor and leaving a mark on the same spot of their own bodies. Ingailor was the last, placing a pink handprint on Kovo's chest and then one on his own. The ape bowed his head, acknowledging their ancient agreement. Meilin watching silently, not wanting to break the spell.

"Xanthe," she finally whispered, nodding deferentially to the elders, "would it be okay if I showed them Jhi?"

"Of course!" Xanthe said. "We would be honored."

Meilin brought the panda out, and Jhi emerged right over a small bush of round mushrooms, squashing them flat and letting out an iridescent pink-green cloud of spores. The panda looked around in surprise, then saw Meilin and bounded over, making a groaning sound that Meilin recognized as the sign of Jhi's purest joy. Meilin threw her arms around her closest friend, breathing in the eucalyptus smell of Jhi's fur, somehow constant through all of the panda's appearings and disappearings. Immediately Jhi was covered in color, from the moist tip of her nose to the soles of her feet. She looked delighted by it.

Conor summoned Briggan, and the wolf was soon

painted as well, though due to his thicker fur the color appeared only at the tips, giving him a shimmering aura. Briggan nuzzled Conor joyously, and Conor buried his face in his friend's fur. Then they seemed to simultaneously remember where they were and got to their feet. The people of Phos Astos were watching them silently, smiles on their faces. Even Kovo's mouth split into something that might have been a smirk.

"Let us rejoice tonight!" Ingailor called. "We have once again defeated the Many, and Great Beasts have come to Phos Astos."

As the cheer died down, Jhi's stomach growled.

Xanthe scrutinized the panda's belly, and then she, too, threw her arms around Jhi. "It took me a moment to realize what that strange sound was," she said. "You must all be starving. Come to my house. We'll feast!"

"This isn't precisely what I'd call a feast, not exactly," Conor said through tight lips.

"Speak for yourself," Meilin said. "I'm enjoying it immensely." She lifted her bowl to her lips and downed a huge mouthful of food, smacking her lips in satisfaction. The food was strangely tasty, considering it consisted of boiled mushroom cubes and some kelp-like black weed. Though they looked the same, some of the mushrooms were peppery and some were sweet. Meilin had Conor on one side, but she'd spent most of the meal talking to Xanthe's uncle on the other. His job was to distinguish and combine the various flavors.

Once they'd eaten, Xanthe escorted the group through a series of passageways, up into some mushroom towers and out through others, until they were at the far side of Phos Astos. Once there, she asked them to bring their spirit animals into passive state, as they'd have to climb slender rope ladders to reach her clan's sleeping quarters. Kovo was the last to go into his dormant state, giving the city a longing glance over his shoulder before he did. The ape had enjoyed the adoration he'd gotten from the Sadreans.

They climbed up more braided ropes that led to three ledges carved in the cavern's rock walls. At the top, they plopped to the ground to rest. Once they were ready, Xanthe led the companions up the last few paces to a free-standing mushroom tower. An open portal fed to a dim interior room. As they entered, Sadrean children leaped down from rows of beds that had been cut out of the sides of the mushroom. They peered shyly from behind Xanthe.

Tiny pale faces with giant pink eyes—Sadrean children were surprisingly adorable, Meilin thought.

"Some of these are blood relatives and some lost their parents, like I once did," Xanthe explained. "But we're all brothers and sisters now."

"War makes orphans everywhere," Takoda said. He tousled the hair of one of the little girls, who patted it down furiously. Takoda messed it up all over again, and this time she broke into a giggling smile. Xanthe's brothers and sisters soon got over their shyness and surrounded the upsiders, touching their garments curiously and asking dozens of questions about life on the surface.

"Let's give them some space," Xanthe finally told her siblings. "My new friends have had a long journey, and they're very tired."

Xanthe carved a path through her siblings and led Meilin, Conor, and Takoda to the rear of the chamber, where she pointed to four empty bunks carved into the rounded wall. "Have as long a rest as you need. You all deserve it."

"I guess it's hard to say 'I'll wake you in the morning' when there's no morning, huh?" Conor said.

"We have a water clock to keep time," Xanthe said. "It's night on the surface right now, actually."

Meilin, Conor, and Takoda slotted their few belongings into cubbies at the foot of their bunks and settled in. Xanthe disappeared for a moment and returned with soft, shimmering black blankets. At first the blanket felt clammy over Meilin's body, but soon it warmed and turned supple. She would sleep just fine.

"Good night," Meilin said to the others as she slid into the bunk.

"I guess it is night," Takoda sleepily responded. "Not that it matters down here. It's a striking shift in perspective. What a marvelous opportunity for self-reflection."

"Sure . . ." Meilin said, voice already weakening as she drifted off, ". . . absolutely marvelous." *Good night, Rollan*, she mouthed to herself, wondering where he was.

Meilin dreamed of Jhi. She'd once had a poisoned bond with the panda, but ever since she'd been cured, Jhi was with her every sleeping moment. Sometimes the dreams were about Meilin's life—her childhood in Zhong, memories of her father or, more distantly, her mother. But other times she dreamed of places she had never been, places that must have been part of Jhi's memories instead. They'd wander into a cloudy forest of bamboo, with giant sloths swaying in the treetops, creatures that no longer existed on Erdas.

This was one of those nights. Meilin wandered that familiar dream forest, listening to the wind in the trees. Jhi was leading the way. Well, Jhi was more ambling the way, wandering among the stems, selecting the youngest shoots and passing every other one back for Meilin to eat. She ate them happily as she stared into the clouds—they tasted slightly spicy, like chives.

The openness of the dream space was such a pleasant break from sky-less Sadre. One of the clouds looked a little like Rollan. Well, not exactly, but it had the same goofy chin. *Jhi*, Meilin called in the dream, *come see Rollan!*

But Jhi wasn't there anymore. Meilin whirled in the bamboo forest. The beauty of her surroundings had turned ominous. She was alone.

Meilin checked her arm, but the tattoo wasn't there—Jhi wasn't passive, but missing. Panic coursing through her, she ran heedlessly through the forest, calling out Jhi's name. Leaves caught and dragged at her hair, scratching her arms and face. There were no monsters or terrors here, but all the same Meilin felt a sinister kind of fear at being so alone. She crashed through a thicket of bamboo, and suddenly she was in open black space, falling slowly down a chasm.

She felt her spine wrench and twist as she fell—

—and woke up screaming. Meilin sat up, gasping and soaked in sweat. The wrenching pain came once again, and it took all of Meilin's will not to give in to the torment and buckle over. Marshaling her training, she made herself stand. The terrible pain ebbed, leaving her a shred of control over her senses. The first thing she did was roll up her sleeve and check her arm for Jhi's tattoo. It was there. She hadn't lost Jhi in the real world.

It dawned on Meilin that someone was shrieking, had been shrieking since she woke up. She fell into a fighter's crouch, staring around in alarm.

It wasn't a person making the sound, she realized, but more like the anguished hiss of steam leaving a kettle. The screamers. The alarm had been tripped.

"Conor! Takoda!" she said. But their beds were empty. She whirled, and found they all were vacant, rimmed in their usual phosphorescent pink-green. The incessant whine of the screamers continued. Between that noise and her painful awakening, Meilin was finding it hard to get her thoughts into any order. She clamped her hands over her ears and gritted her teeth so she wouldn't start screaming herself.

Meilin grabbed her quarterstaff and staggered toward the exit, shaking her head in hopes of clearing it. Once she was out of the tight confines of the sleeping chamber, she summoned Jhi. It took longer for the panda to arrive, but when she finally did, Meilin calmed. Jhi startled in the dim light and blaring noise, then Meilin saw her ears wag, and the noise suddenly stopped.

They were surrounded by a sphere of stillness.

"Jhi," Meilin whispered, "I didn't know you could do that."

Jhi nodded but looked at her glassily. Meilin felt a strange and uncomfortable distance between them. She wanted to ask what was wrong, but there wasn't time. "Come," she said, a hand on Jhi's back. "We need to find Conor and Takoda!"

Jhi didn't answer. When Meilin looked at her, she realized why.

The panda was staring out at the lights of Phos Astos. At first Meilin thought the lights were shimmering, but she quickly realized what was happening: The beautiful city was under assault. The Many were crawling over the mushroom towers like a plague of insects, making ripples in the glowing light. They climbed senselessly, moving up the mushrooms in pulsating waves, many of them tumbling to their deaths. But an ever-growing swarm was ready to take their place. The far half of the city was overrun—Meilin saw terrified families emerge from their homes, only to fall under the onslaught. She watched in horror as one of the ghoulish monsters broke into the spider pen and began eating the small animals—another entered the weavers' quarters, exiting with blood on his clawed hands.

Jhi groaned and pointed her paw at the ceiling.

Ghouls were falling like rain.

The Many had managed to navigate the warren of

tunnels to the updraft entrance. A long line of them slowly descended in the lazy hot air, thronging in one pale groaning mass at the first net before spilling over into the next. From there they spread out hungrily into Phos Astos, swarming the city like ants on a bean cake.

Meilin shook off her horror. There was a big fight to come, and terror would do her no good. Beside her, one of Xanthe's siblings slipped past, grabbed a braided rope without losing any speed, and disappeared over the side of the mushroom, down to the next ledge.

"Where are you going?" Meilin called after her. But there was no answer.

What she did hear was the howl of a wolf from one of the ledges below. Briggan and Conor were already out and fighting. "Jhi, get ready!" Meilin cried. "We're joining them!"

She sprinted toward the braided rope ladder and grabbed it, allowing her momentum to kick her legs over the edge. Her hands held on tight to the rope and she spun, sliding down without losing any momentum.

While she was in the air, she did something she and Jhi had worked on during her months in Zhong: She called Jhi into her passive state as she contacted the rope, then sped down the length, where she quickly summoned the panda again. They'd gotten the high-speed summoning down to a science, but this time her bond seemed to shudder under the stress. A fraying pain whipped into the core of Meilin.

The distraction of it made her miss her target; girl and panda tumbled right onto the coarse fur of Briggan's back.

The wolf yelped in surprise and pivoted, his mouth in a snarl. When he saw who he'd cushioned, his tongue lolled out in happiness.

The four of them were alone on a broad ledge of rock. Conor stood at the lip and stared over, his ax out and ready.

"Conor!" Meilin cried.

He turned, surprised. His expression softened when he saw his friend, but then tightened back up with worry. "Another wave's coming—Meilin, get ready!"

Meilin didn't need to ask what he meant: A ghostly-white hand appeared at the lip of the ledge, followed by another and another. With hideous grunting sounds, the arms and heads of the ghastly creatures appeared. Briggan lunged, one of the monsters' limbs instantly crunching within his jaws. With a flick of his head, he flung the ghoul over the side.

But more of the Many were appearing, and two of them soon had their long-nailed fingers around Briggan's tail. The wolf danced and kicked, trying to free himself. Caught off-guard, one fell away—only to meet Jhi's paw. With one mighty swipe, the panda sent the creature skittering across the ledge and into the void. Another of the Many got to its feet, only to face Conor's ax, which swung through the pink-green light and slammed into its face. With a shriek of pain, the monster staggered backward—following the last one right over the edge. It fell screaming into the open air, the sound lasting a full second before it cut off in a sickening gargle.

Four more of the Many appeared, and rather than falling into her customary fighting crouch, Meilin leaped into the air, whipping her quarterstaff in a wide, singing arc, cracking into the neck of one monster and bowling it into the next and the next, so that all three went screaming into the darkness.

"Good one!" Conor cried.

"My bond with Jhi . . ." Meilin said breathlessly, joining Conor at the edge as he stomped on the hands of the Many whenever they appeared. "Something happened. It's weaker—"

"I felt it, too," Conor said. "Then I heard the alarm. There must not have been time to repair the dam." He grunted as he lifted the hand of a particularly strong creature and flung it over the edge.

Meilin remembered her remorse over drowning the horde and cursed her own soft heart. "Where's Takoda?" she asked.

This wave of attackers finished, Conor managed a wicked grin. "Look below."

Jhi and Meilin cautiously leaned over the edge and peered down. There, on a wider ledge directly below theirs, Takoda and Kovo were facing their own batch of the Many. Because their position was lower, they confronted a much larger throng—Conor and Meilin had been fighting only the trickle that made it past the powerful ape. Takoda had mounted Kovo's back and had his slender arms wrapped around the gorilla's neck.

Kovo had his arms held out wide and was turning in low circles, flailing any of the Many that were unfortunate enough to fall within his reach and sending them screaming over the edge. Any time Kovo windmilled his arms, only the ghouls at the far sides of the ledge survived to climb up toward Conor and Meilin. Before her eyes, Meilin saw one of them emerge, only to become a rag toy in Briggan's powerful teeth.

"Any sign of Xanthe?" Meilin asked.

Conor shook his head. "She must be off defending another part of the city."

"How do we get out of here?" Meilin asked. When the head of one of the Many appeared over the edge, she brought her quarterstaff down in a fierce overhead blow, knocking the creature senseless. It tumbled away, arms pinwheeling through the air.

"We've got to get down to Takoda's ledge," Conor said. "It's our only hope. The cavern floor is below it. Once we get that far, maybe we can find a passage that will take us away from here. Only problem is this." Conor held up the climbing rope, which had been severed in the fighting.

"Wait. What do you mean, 'away from here'? We can't abandon Phos Astos—it's the last standing city in Sadre!"

"Have you seen the destruction out there? Phos Astos is lost," Conor said. "If this many attackers are at the edge where we are, there's no way the Sadreans will hold out at the center. Our dying here won't help anything."

Meilin's mouth pressed into a scowl. She'd seen war. She'd once witnessed her own city fall to invaders, and had been forced to flee and become a refugee from her home.

This was worse. It wasn't occupation; it was annihilation.

This strange and wonderful place—this city of light—was about to blink out forever. And there was nothing she could do about it. Her eyes stung with frustration. How had she come to be here? She'd left Greenhaven to help the world *rebuild*. And now she was only witnessing destruction.

"It's thirty feet down to the next ledge," Meilin said brusquely, wiping her tears away before Conor could see them. "If we jump, we break our legs. We have to scale down the rock face."

Conor shook his head. "Kovo managed it, but only just. And he's an *ape*. I don't think we'd have a chance of making it down."

Meilin peered over the edge again, thinking. She nodded. "I have a plan. Don't ask what it is, just watch."

"What is—" Conor asked, then stopped with a sheepish look.

Meilin stepped back from the lip, calling Jhi into passive state as she did. Again, she felt the wrenching pain of her frayed bond whipping through her core. She let one of the Many climb all the way onto the ledge. The moment it was on its feet, it rushed Meilin, yellow fingernails outstretched and mouth bared. The spiral on its forehead throbbed and twisted as Meilin reared her staff back. But rather than strike the monster with its length, she thrust with its tip. The pole struck the creature in its chest and sent it flying backward.

Meilin followed after, pole-vaulting over the edge with the tumbling monster. She kicked out with both her feet so they hit its chest, and then she was surfing on the tumbling body. The creature's back worked like a kite in the open air, slowing Meilin's descent. When it struck the ledge, she rolled free.

She'd have to leave it to trust that Conor was following the same plan, as the moment she hit the lower ledge Meilin was surrounded by the gnashing teeth and claws of the Many. She managed to get her staff out in time to cuff the chin of a ghastly monster who was about to sink its teeth into her shoulder. It reeled, bowling over two of its companions.

"Takoda!" Meilin called.

Takoda didn't react; he had enough to worry about, struggling to keep himself on Kovo's shoulders as the gorilla pivoted and swung his meaty arms. Kovo's technique was still working, keeping a circle of stone floor clear around him, but even he was tiring.

As she battled, Meilin heard Conor drop to the ledge beside her, followed by a popping sound as Briggan reappeared. She wished she could summon Jhi, but the ledge was too narrow for all their spirit animals.

"This horde won't end. We need to drop down as soon as we have an opening!" Meilin cried.

Kovo didn't respond—he just stepped quickly to the edge and dropped over into the darkness, taking a surprised and shrieking Takoda with him.

Meilin and Conor ran up to the lip of the ledge and, after peeking over and seeing there was only a few yards' drop, stepped over.

As she landed, Phos Astos came into view. The sight was enough to confirm that the last city of Sadre was definitely lost. The scrambling forms of the Many riddled the giant mushrooms like parasites, attacking whoever they could find. Their pale bodies shone in the pink-green light. More streamed down in the updraft, a torrent of slavering ghouls that cascaded into the city like an unholy waterfall.

The sight of the devastation took Meilin's breath away, but Conor was instantly on his feet, running toward the tunnel that led out of the city. Without losing any momentum, he whipped out his ax just in time to take down one of the Many that came too close. Meilin fell into a sprint, right behind Briggan.

Conor veered to one side, and Meilin realized what he was heading for. At the base of the last mushroom before the cavern wall, Xanthe and Ingailor were locked in combat against a gibbering throng of enemies.

Back to back, they had bright crystal maces in their hands and were wielding the glowing rocks like dual swords; wherever the shining weapons went, the Many recoiled. Their slices and parries left broad arcs of light in the air. But their enemies were increasing in number, and as they did, they grew more aggressive. The tunnel to the slate plain was soon blocked by a horde of creatures.

There was a rush of black at the edge of Meilin's vision as Kovo charged past, his meaty hands and feet impacting the ground with great rumbling thuds that sent tremors through her gut. The gorilla furiously set upon the Many, pounding them from above. Takoda still clung desperately to his back.

Scrambling after him, Meilin watched helplessly as Xanthe lost her footing and tumbled before the pressing mass of the Many. For an anguished moment she disappeared entirely from view. Then the girl reappeared, struggling against one of the Many who had her scalp in its grasp. It yanked her head back to expose her slender, pale neck.

"No!" Meilin cried out. But she was too far away to save her new friend.

Ingailor, however, was not. He threw himself onto the monster, ripping it from Xanthe. But the beast twisted in his grasp, and in the space of one horrifying split-second it had sunk its yellow teeth into his neck. Another took advantage of the opening to pounce, landing on Ingailor's shoulders. The Sadrean elder fell into the horde and did not come back up.

For a horrified second, Xanthe stared at the space where the elder had fallen, her face frozen in utter shock. A monster leaped from the side, long-nailed fingers ready to swipe.

By then, Kovo and Takoda had arrived. The ape pummeled the creatures approaching Xanthe while Takoda reached down from his vantage point on Kovo's back. He grabbed the back of Xanthe's shift and hauled her up in front of him. Meilin streaked to their side and heard Takoda yell to Xanthe: "Where should we go?"

But the girl was in shock. Her mouth was slack as she stared at the space where Ingailor had so recently stood, now crawling with monsters. It was all she could do to hold on to Takoda's arms.

"Head for the exit tunnel!" Meilin yelled while she fended off another attacker. A low roundhouse sent him staggering to the ground. "There's no other option!"

Fatigued and struggling under the weight of two riders, Kovo tottered and nearly fell. But he righted himself and lurched toward the tunnel.

Xanthe managed to find the wits to hold her crystal mace in front of Kovo's forehead. The glow helped keep their enemies at bay. Conor and Briggan tucked themselves into the open space behind Kovo, and Meilin took up the rear, swiping her quarterstaff at any enemies that got too close.

Though she couldn't risk turning her head to see where they were going, Meilin felt the ground slope slightly, and then cool, dank air washed over her flushed cheeks. The glowing lights of Phos Astos narrowed to an oval, then a point as they fought their way deep into the exit tunnel.

Jabbering with fury, the Many pressed after them, but Meilin could no longer be flanked in the narrow confines. She went on the offensive, bludgeoning any creature that came near. While she fought off their enemies, she heard Xanthe's voice from somewhere behind her: "There's a secret rope here. There, tucked into the crevice!"

Then she heard two rapid pops as Kovo and Briggan disappeared. Someone was climbing nearby. She saw a braided rope enter her vision, even as she sliced her staff at an attacker. "You'll be the last one up," Conor called after her. "As soon as there's an opening, climb this."

She heard the rope creak as the others ascended behind her. Then she made a final stand, knocking one attacker into the next hard enough that the two bowled down the one behind. Meilin used the opportunity to grope in the darkness for . . . the rope! She caught the knotted cable and scrambled upward, her arms burning with exhaustion. Once she'd gone a ways up, she felt a familiar grip on her shoulders as Conor helped her the rest of the way.

Meilin lay on the tunnel floor, panting, while Conor pulled the rope back up. Then he collapsed next to her. Takoda lay in a similar state of exhaustion on her other side. Meilin turned her head in time to see his tattoo quiver and then disappear. Kovo appeared, sitting on the stone floor. She summoned Jhi, and Conor did the same with Briggan.

Xanthe had huddled herself against the wall, her head pressed tight against her knees. Jhi ambled over and sat by her side, resting her soft, furry back against Xanthe's. The panda always knew who was in the most need.

For a long moment, all they did was catch their breath in the darkness.

As soon as she could, Meilin sat up and faced Xanthe. She lay a hand on the Sadrean girl's elbow. "Xanthe? Are you okay?"

Xanthe tried to nod, but she was shaking too violently. She jerked back and pressed against the rock wall, away from Meilin and Jhi.

"Are we safe for now?" Meilin asked.

Xanthe nodded again, though the words that tumbled out of her mouth were: "Phos Astos is gone."

"I'm sorry about Ingailor," Conor said.

She glared at him. "They're *all* dead," she snapped. "Not just him. My family! All of them! Dead because of those mindless monsters!"

Conor shrank away, his face blanching even in the shadows.

Takoda knelt beside Xanthe, and to Meilin's surprise he took her trembling frame fully in his arms. "I know," the boy said. "You must be in so much pain. I'm sorry." His face was full of both yearning sadness and affection.

Kovo slowly turned so he could no longer see Takoda and Xanthe. His scarlet eyes clouded, and his face twisted with something Meilin was slow to recognize. Kovo looked . . . jealous. It was an emotion she'd never have expected in the gorilla.

It seemed like Kovo had surprised himself, too. He breathed heavily for a moment, then sat back on his haunches and very deliberately closed his eyes, hands balled into tight fists at his side.

"Xanthe," Meilin said, "we may be safe in this tunnel for now, but I can't imagine we will be for long. I can hear the Many congregating down there."

"Give her a second!" Takoda snapped.

Meilin recoiled, stung.

Xanthe pulled out of Takoda's embrace. "No, Meilin is right. We need to get moving."

"The question is where," Conor said.

"No, *that* is not a question," Xanthe said. Her face was as white as bone, leached of even its faint color.

"What do you mean?"

165

"This tunnel goes south, but it branches soon," Xanthe said. "There are indeed decisions to be made, but there's no question of our eventual destination. Our last city is destroyed. My family . . . We cannot let that be in vain."

"The Evertree," Meilin said. "We have to go to the Evertree."

"Yes," Xanthe said. She determinedly wiped her tears away. "Look." She pointed to the ceiling of the tunnel. Wide cracks lined it, and within each was the skinny tendril of a root.

"That couldn't possibly be . . ." Meilin said. "The Evertree is miles away."

"The roots of the Evertree are far wider than the tree itself," said Xanthe. "The Evertree *is* Erdas, and we are it. But these roots, too, are dwindling. Even a few days ago, they filled these crevices. But now they have shrunken—the tree has retracted them, because it's sick."

"We must cure it," Meilin said.

"Then we'll need to destroy the Wyrm," Xanthe said. "The Wyrm is where the parasites are emerging from. The Wyrm is the scourge sickening the Evertree. If the tree dies, the bonds between humans and spirit animals will disappear entirely—and worse."

"Look!" Conor said. "The root!"

In front of Meilin's eyes, the root lining the ceiling began to quiver, echoed by an aching throb in Meilin's spine. Then the quivering intensified, as did the throb. "Oh no, oh no—" Meilin said.

Then it happened. Like the blast of a horn right in her ear, pain ripped through her, obliterating every other sensation. She buckled under it, and saw through the flashing agony that Takoda and Conor were experiencing the same torment.

She screamed and curled into a fetal position on the floor. Around her she heard, not just the cries of her friends, but sharp whimpers from Jhi, whining howls from Briggan, and anguished grunts from Kovo. Then, slowly, the pain around Meilin's spine released. She sat up, drenched in sweat, and looked around her. Briggan's and Jhi's eyes were rimmed in fearful white, and Kovo's face was scrunched down at the pain he'd been through.

"What just happened to you all?" Xanthe asked quietly.

Meilin looked into Jhi's eyes, and it was like staring at a stranger. "Our spirit animal bonds just . . . frayed," Meilin panted. "That's the only way I can describe it."

"And look," Xanthe said, pointing at the crevices in the ceiling. "The Evertree's roots retracted as the pain came."

Meilin heard Kovo snort, then turned to see him sitting before Takoda, signing. The ape made a rumbling sound of complaint.

"Kovo says he's noticed it, too," Takoda said. "He can't sense my thoughts the way he used to."

"I'd call that a good thing," Conor said, looking suspiciously at the ape. He stood with a grunt and lit a torch. The scant light of the tunnel became a full blaze.

Meilin risked a look at Kovo. She found he was already watching her, his scarlet eyes gleaming with furious intensity. It was hard to know what he was thinking, but one thing was unmistakable: Kovo was under no one's control. He knew more than any of them about what was happening, and they were all at his mercy.

With a gruff snort, Kovo turned and headed down the tunnel. Toward Nilo. Toward the Wyrm.

14

AMBUSH

ROLLAN TUMBLED IN THE DIM LIGHT OF DAWN. HE landed on his hands and knees and screamed as he struggled to escape his mysterious attacker. Essix relied on vision, not smell, so in the dim light she must have been caught as unawares as Rollan. He heard a rush of wind and a surprised shriek as the falcon swooped to his side. As soon as she landed, Essix was back in the air again. Another raptor screamed, and the vise-like clamp on the back of Rollan's thigh eased.

He freed himself and whirled in confusion—the sounds of his foes were coming from all directions. Though the mountains still blocked the dawn, a few scraps of light had iced the dewy grasses only a few yards away. That's where Rollan staggered, knowing he and his friends would have a better chance of defending themselves if they could see who they were fighting.

Along the way he stumbled into Abeke. She nodded in the direction he was moving, and wordlessly followed.

Anda and Tellun were at their side by the time Rollan got to the open grassland.

A handsome bearded man emerged from the darkness, clad in a black tunic. Even in the predawn light, Rollan could see that there was a spiral on his forehead, where the strange creature writhed beneath the skin.

"Hello, Rollan and Abeke," the man said calmly. "It has been some time. Can't say I've missed you."

"Zerif!" Abeke said, her bow in hand. "What happened to you?"

"Something *wonderful*," Zerif answered. "Though far beyond your understanding. The Wyrm awakens, and I awaken with it."

Rollan noted that the man still carried his oily charm, but Conor had been right: Something was off about Zerif. His eyes were a bit too wild. His smile was a bit too stretched.

"And this must be the boy who has summoned Tellun," Zerif continued, turning to Anda. "What is about to happen to you can either be painful or mercifully quick. The amount you will suffer is your choice, but the outcome is not. Tellun will be mine."

In response, Tellun bowed his noble head—not in deference, but in preparation to charge. He raised one hoof and pressed it to the earth, like a runner taking his mark. But then he paused.

Something emerged from the shadows behind Zerif.

It was a large serpent, as thick as a tree trunk, with a broad, triangular head. Her wide, slitted eyes had a manic tilt to them, and as she came into the full light she reared back and opened her black hood. Fear filled Rollan's mouth with a foul, bitter taste, and his skin felt like rubber. He'd met this cobra before, during the war. Of all the opponents they'd faced, cruel Gerathon was the one who most often stalked his dreams.

"Gerathon," Abeke said bitterly. *"You've* bowed to this fool?"

Abeke knew what she was doing: Gerathon had always been a haughty, stubborn creature, with a definite bent for killing humans. It might work to pit her pride against Zerif. But the cobra's triangular face remained impassive as she turned her merciless gaze on them. Rollan knew from experience that, although they were a dozen feet away, they were still within striking range of the cobra's fangs.

Rollan had his dagger out, ready to dodge and counterattack, but Essix chirped to stop him.

Tellun stepped forward, approaching the serpent. Rollan's heart was in his mouth as he watched the elk stride calmly in front of the coiled snake and go perfectly still, head lowered.

Staring right into Gerathon's slitted eyes, Tellun worked his way closer. Though information seemed to pass between the beasts, Tellun apparently didn't get the response he'd expected. Gerathon lunged, hissing, and the elk sprang to one side, all four legs tucking under him in the air.

Beside Gerathon, another form emerged from the darkness—an eagle, slightly larger and stockier than Essix, with a sharp and noble prow.

A new fear pricked at Rollan's neck as Halawir looked hungrily at Essix. The falcon would be in for the fight of her life if it came to aerial combat. "Stay near," he whispered to her.

Rollan heard Abeke's bow creak, and knew she was readying for battle. "I don't know what your plan is," Abeke called to Zerif, "but you won't have Tellun as part of it."

"Are you so sure?" Zerif spat. "He'll have no say in the matter."

"Prepare," Abeke told Rollan and Anda through the side of her mouth.

Gone were the days of allowing Zerif to call the first shot; Abeke gave no warning before letting her arrow fly. He dodged to one side just in time, and the arrow thudded into something beyond the edge of the dawn's light—something that trumpeted in anger. The ground rumbled as the furious beast surged forward. It was Dinesh, the mighty elephant thudding into the crisp light, rage in his eyes and a comparatively puny arrow shaft sticking out of his flank.

Trembling, Anda took an involuntary step backward. "We have to run!" he whispered. "We have no chance against them."

Fear had the opposite effect on Abeke; she gave a battle cry and summoned Uraza. Instantly, the powerful cat was twining itself around her feet, growling as she prepared for the fight.

But then Zerif ripped open the front of his tunic, revealing three more tattoos riding the muscles of his chest—a boar, a ram, and a polar bear. One by one the tattoos flashed and disappeared, until three more Great Beasts stood before them: Rumfuss the Boar, with his wide, flat head and pointed shredding tusks, chilly hatred in his expression; Arax the Ram, all wiry hair and bounding energy, bitter anger flashing in his eyes; and Suka the Polar Bear, the largest of them all, with pure white fur. The polar bear's black lips pulled back to reveal a row of powerful teeth.

As one, the beasts leveled their hostile gazes on the companions. Zerif had them all under his command; there was no doubting it.

"Anda, run!" Rollan ordered. "We'll hold them off as long as we can!"

Essix launched herself at Zerif, but Halawir unfurled his great wings and sprang to meet the falcon. He hooked his sharp beak around one of Essix's talons, and the two crashed together in the air, tumbling, beaks snapping and clawed feet gouging. They flew higher as they went, shreds of feathers floating down.

Though Rollan was desperate to keep his eyes on Essix, he had plenty to worry about on the ground. With Arax, Rumfuss, and Suka at his side, Zerif charged Tellun. Arax pulled ahead first, brow lowered to the horizon line so his great curving horns were parallel to the ground.

But Tellun held his ground, four legs planted deep in the earth, antlers lowered in defense. They looked spindly compared to Arax's densely curled horns.

Anda had started to flee, but when it was clear Tellun was making a stand, he reversed course and raced to his side. He was still yards away when the two Great Beasts made impact. With a horrifying crunch of breaking bones, they went down in a cloud of geysering dirt.

When the dust cleared, Rollan saw Tellun staggering to his feet. A fragment of antler was on the ground, but the elk was otherwise unharmed. Apparently those antlers weren't as spindly as Rollan had thought.

Arax was splayed out on his side but soon leaped back up, preparing to charge again.

Now it was Rumfuss's turn to attack. His short legs didn't allow him to get nearly the momentum Arax had, but he scissored his tusked head from side to side as he went, ready to slice anything that got in his path. The impact with Arax had spun Tellun sideways, and the boar would soon catch him broadside. When Rumfuss hit, Tellun would be gored.

If not for Uraza. The leopard had been silently circling the field since the attack began, and launched herself with the speed of one of Abeke's arrows, hurtling through the air to strike Rumfuss's flank. Her claws sank into the boar's tough hide. They did little damage but held like burrs, and Uraza's weight fishtailed Rumfuss to one side, crashing leopard and boar into the dirt. When Gerathon streaked toward the pair, Abeke loosed an arrow that embedded into the snake's tail. Gerathon hissed, hesitating long enough for Uraza to scramble to her feet and make a desperate leap to the side. Gerathon's fangs sank into the dirt where Uraza had been only moments before. Another arrow and the serpent was pinned at the hood, flailing as she tried to extract herself from the rocky soil.

That still left a man, an elephant, and a polar bear for the others to contend with, with Arax preparing to rejoin the attack. While Tellun settled into a defensive stance, Rollan took up a position next to Abeke, with Anda behind him.

"Let's do this," Rollan said grimly.

Abeke nodded resolutely.

"I'm afraid I'm not much help as a warrior," Anda said.

"Don't apologize," Abeke said sharply. "Just fight as you can!"

Anda cast a glance to Tellun, and Rollan was surprised to see a lack of fear on the boy's face, though surely he had to be aware of the hopelessness of their fight.

Dinesh led the charge. As the massive, trumpeting animal bore down on them, Rollan knew they had only two options: Get out of the way or die.

The companions' hasty defensive line scattered as they tumbled to either side. Even Tellun didn't dare stand up to the massive beast. He leaped directly away from Dinesh, looking over his shoulder to make sure the elephant gave chase. Only the elk could hope to match Dinesh once he got up to speed. The fleet leader of the Great Beasts was soon leading Dinesh away from the companions. Rollan could hear the crash and clatter of the life-or-death chase as they hurtled away.

A few yards off, Uraza was facing the impossible task of simultaneously holding off Rumfuss and Arax. While her assailants circled and lunged, Uraza growled and dodged, making harassing jabs with her claws as she tried to keep the beasts distracted and buy them all time.

Somewhere in the sky above, Essix's shrieks matched Halawir's screeches as more broken feathers glided down to the earth.

Meanwhile, arms crossed over his chest, Zerif calmly took in Rollan, Abeke, and Anda where they lay sprawled in the dirt. "I will claim three Great Beasts today. My job is nearly done."

"You will not have Uraza!" Abeke said, spitting blood as she got to her feet and dusted herself off. With the leopard present, she was even more agile than usual, regaining her feet in one springing motion. "I'd bring her back into tattoo form long before you could take her."

"Sadly, you're right," Zerif said, leaning nonchalantly against Suka's flank. The possessed polar bear didn't even seem to notice the man next to her, her smoldering eyes fixed on the fleeing elk. "I'll have to kill you first. Though I wonder if Tellun has the same protection." His eyes fell on Anda. "Tell me, plainsboy, you only just summoned the Great Elk. Have you mastered *his* dormant state?"

Anda didn't answer, but his wide, fearful eyes confirmed plenty.

Zerif's mouth split into an oily grin. "So much of my life lately has been about good timing."

Rollan readied his dagger, clenching his sweaty fingers over its leather grip as he kept his eyes on Suka. Powerful and agile—even a normal polar bear was nothing Rollan and Abeke could contend with without the aid of their spirit animals . . . and Uraza and Essix had their own life-or-death battles. Favoring his good leg, Rollan edged closer to Anda.

"Suka," Zerif commanded, "kill the plainsboy first."

Suka bared her sharp yellow teeth and took off toward Anda, starting slow and lumbering but soon at lethal speed. The boy scrambled backward and tumbled, grinding his body through the dirt in his haste to get away. Abeke loosed an arrow at the bear, but cursed as it did nothing to slow her. She readied another, but she would have no time to shoot before Suka reached Anda. Rollan threw himself forward and tried to slash at the bear with his dagger, but the blade was slowed by her thick pelt and only barely nicked Suka's skin. The polar bear continued unimpeded.

With one great swipe of her claw, the boy was lying prone on the ground. With another swipe, his body tumbled and rolled and came to rest beside a tree.

Abeke got another arrow off, and this one made contact, hitting Suka in the flank. The polar bear roared in pain. But it was too little, too late. Suka laid one strong paw on Anda's chest where he lay still and opened her massive jaw to finish him off.

Anda's life would have ended right then—if it hadn't been for Tellun. Tree branches snapped sharply as the elk burst over a rise, head bowed, heading straight for the polar bear who had dared harm his boy. Caught by surprise, Suka took Tellun's antlers hard in the flank and fell over, rolling in the dirt.

Tellun stood over the moaning Anda, antlers lowered protectively. The elk was bleeding from many places, including one particularly nasty wound on his backside that must have come from Dinesh's tusks. Rollan noticed that Dinesh had not followed Tellun and felt a glimmer of hope: Could it be that Tellun had actually defeated him?

Zerif had taken advantage of the distraction to creep up undetected. Tellun was facing Suka, ribs shuddering with exhaustion, foamy spittle dripping from his mouth. Abeke worked busily to get a third arrow notched. With his wounded leg, Rollan was too far from the fight to reach them in time. "Watch out, Tellun!" he cried.

Zerif was upon the elk before Tellun could whirl to face him. That moment of advantage was all he needed. With vision sharpened by his affinity with Essix, Rollan watched Zerif unstopper a vial and splash something gray and squirming right onto the elk's gashed cheek.

For a moment, the leader of the Great Beasts was frozen in shock. Then he frantically slashed his head from side to side, trying to get the creature off. It continued to wriggle up his head, though, and as it did Tellun seemed to realize what was happening. He looked down at Anda, sorrow joining bewilderment on the elk's face.

"No!" Anda cried. The boy managed to raise himself to his forearms just in time to watch Tellun's expression change to anguished horror as the creature disappeared under his skin. The elk's eyes went milky, then bright.

He turned coldly away from Anda and stood at attention, ready for orders.

From Zerif.

"Tellun?" Anda called, eyes wet with tears.

"Slay the boy," Zerif commanded.

Without even a moment of hesitation, Tellun lowered his head, preparing to charge in with his sharp antlers.

Rollan peered around in desperation. Essix was locked in combat with Halawir, and Uraza was still busy with Arax and Rumfuss, breathing heavily with exhaustion. Anda lay motionless on the ground, paralyzed by shock.

It seemed hopeless.

Until he heard a whizzing sound, right over his shoulder, as a spear appeared in Tellun's leg.

Rollan watched in astonishment as the elk fell. It wasn't a mortal wound, but it was crippling; the elk struggled and failed to get up, neck muscles standing out as he thrashed and struggled. Tellun was out of commission.

Some of the hunters from Anda's tribe must have followed them! Rollan whirled, hoping to see Anda's parents had come up behind them.

Instead, striding out of the dawn mists, was a stranger.

Friend or foe, child or adult, it was hard to tell anything, as the mysterious figure wore a long, stiff crimson cloak. Even if there hadn't been a hood hanging low over his head, a curious mask—a single white plate, like one huge scale of a reptile—covered his features. The stranger strode forward fearlessly, the fingers of one leather-gloved hand flexing and unflexing.

"Stop right there!" Zerif called.

Tellun was baying in agony from the spear. Rollan had never heard such a terrible noise.

The red figure continued striding forward. Though the movement looked effortless, the stranger approached at the speed of a sprint and was soon upon them. To Rollan's shock, he went straight for Suka. The polar bear opened her jaws to strike, but the stranger was too quick. His run turned into a dropkick, and the heel of his boot smacked Suka full in the face. Already weakened, the enormous bear groaned and tumbled to one side, unconscious.

Rollan and Zerif both were frozen in shock at the stranger's amazing strength. Abeke took the opportunity to loose her third arrow, this one right at Zerif. It struck the man in the abdomen, and he doubled over. For a moment he looked at the shaft in astonishment, as if surprised to find himself vulnerable after all. Then—his eyes full of a maniac's zeal—he yanked the arrow back out and threw it to one side, drawing himself back up to his full height.

Abeke's next arrow went to Rumfuss, striking his shoulder. When the boar looked up in surprise, Uraza swiped him in the face. Having freed herself from the arrow, Gerathon arrived and was soon coiled and making feinting strikes with her hooded fangs. Bleeding from the leopard's gashes, Rumfuss returned his attention to Uraza.

Arax was unwatched.

Abeke's desperate shot had left her open to attack. Arax lowered his head and charged. Though Rollan shouted for his friend's attention, it was too late—there was no way Abeke would be able to leap away in time. Once Arax's horns hit her at this speed, death would be instant.

But with one long stride, the red-cloaked stranger was in front of Abeke. As Arax neared, the figure simply held out its hands. Rollan gasped when he realized the stranger meant to *catch* the ram's horns.

With a giant thunderclap of sound, a cloud of soil and rock erupted into the air, like an explosion had gone off beneath the earth. When the cloud settled, Rollan strained his eyes through the dust to see what had happened.

The figure was still on his feet.

But Arax was not.

With superhuman strength, the stranger pressed Arax's horns deeper and deeper into the ground. The ram struggled but was wrenched hard into the soil, neck bending, his possessed eyes now full of fright. Rollan found himself swelling with unexpected pity for the once Great Beast.

Above, Rollan heard Essix shrieking. She wouldn't be able to keep Halawir at bay for much longer. Rumfuss, too, was up and ready to attack again.

"Zerif!" Rollan cried, trying to keep the desperation out of his voice. "Suka and Arax have fallen, and Dinesh has disappeared. Surrender!"

Zerif narrowed his eyes and flicked them to the figure in red. Rollan watched as furious calculations passed behind Zerif's eyes. Finally, the man in black nodded, a scowl twisting his mouth. "You might keep Uraza and Essix today, but I have what I came for. Tellun is mine!"

Zerif parted the rent fabric of his tunic farther, and with a flash and a popping sound, Suka and then Arax disappeared, right under the hands of the masked stranger. Zerif must have called Dinesh from wherever he was trapped, too. All three appeared as tattoos on his chest.

Finally, without a second look at Anda, Tellun himself vanished and appeared as a tattoo crossing Zerif's ribs and up under his arm, his antlers just gracing the hollows of Zerif's collarbone. Anda got one dazed look at the elk emblazoned on the body of his enemy and finally passed out, his eyes rolling white before his head hit the earth.

Zerif kept Rumfuss, Halawir, and Gerathon in active form. The beasts flocked to his side, ready to press the attack.

Abeke soon had another arrow notched and pointed at Zerif's heart. Zerif put one hand out to still her. "Your plainsboy friend will die unless you bandage his wounds now. If you shoot, we will attack."

Abeke's fingers on the arrow shook with tension for a moment, but then she wearily nodded and lowered her bow.

While Zerif headed off toward the forest line, his beasts tailing after him, Uraza and Essix returned to Anda's side.

Once their enemies were out of sight, Abeke dropped her bow and ran to the boy.

Rollan, though, went to the red-cloaked figure. "Thank you for your help," he said warily.

The figure didn't respond, just stood perfectly still, arms folded. Then the shining white mask nodded, catching gleams of the dawn's light.

"What's your name?" Rollan asked.

With one hand, the figure pointed to Anda. The meaning was clear: *Go help your friend.*

Then the red-cloaked stranger took off into the trees, following Zerif. As he went, he recovered his spear from the ground where Suka had disappeared. He inspected the tip, then hefted it, preparing to throw again. Apparently the battle wasn't over for everyone.

Rollan rushed to Anda's side. Abeke was busy dabbing at Anda's face with his own shirt, which she had ripped free to use as a bandage. "He's bleeding a lot. We need to get him to the ship quickly. If we move fast, I think that he'll live."

"His tribe trusted him to us . . ." Rollan said grimly. He squeezed his eyes shut as the full scope of their failure came into focus. He took a ragged breath. "I'll make a stretcher."

As he ran to a nearby fallen tree to strip branches, Rollan's mind raced. Why was Zerif stealing the Great Beasts? How did this gray parasite take over its host, and where did it come from? And who was that masked red figure who had clearly been tailing them as well?

Zerif had mentioned a name when he attacked—the Wyrm. He'd said it was awakening. What did that mean?

While Rollan hacked at branches to start making a stretcher, the question that loomed largest in his mind was also the saddest. How would Anda react when he woke up? Tellun, the greatest of the Great Beasts, the noble elk who'd become his closest companion, had been taken from him.

Though it was heartbreaking to imagine, Rollan sensed that Tellun wasn't all that would be taken from them in the days to come. Not by far.

Eliot Schrefer is the two-time National Book Award Finalist author of *Endangered* and *Threatened*, jungle survival stories about apes. His research for his Great Ape Quartet books has brought him to a bonobo orphanage in Congo and on a boat trek through the waterways of Borneo. *Immortal Guardians* is the second book he's written for the Spirit Animals series.

BOOK TWO:

BROKEN GROUND

Split between two worlds, the team races to stop an
ancient evil. Below, Conor and Meilin must cross a vast
spiderweb, while above, Rollan and Abeke journey to
Stetriol—the kingdom that nearly destroyed Erdas.

scholastic.com/spiritanimals

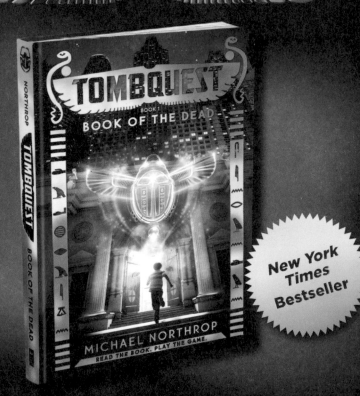